Advent
Nine

Helen Paiba is known a... ... ...c most committed, knowledgeable and acclaimed children's booksellers in Britain. For more than twenty years she owned and ran the Children's Bookshop in Muswell Hill, London, which under her guidance gained a superb reputation for its range of children's books and for the advice available to its customers.

Helen was involved with the Booksellers Association for many years and served on both its Children's Bookselling Group and the Trade Practices Committee. In 1995 she was given honorary life membership of the Booksellers Association of Great Britain and Ireland in recognition of her outstanding services to the association and to the book trade. In the same year the Children's Book Circle (sponsored by Books for Children) honoured her with the Eleanor Farjeon Award, given for distinguished service to the world of children's books.

She retired in 1995 and now lives in London.

Titles available in this series

Funny Stories for Five Year Olds
Magical Stories for Five Year Olds
Animal Stories for Five Year Olds
Adventure Stories for Five Year Olds
Bedtime Stories for Five Year Olds

Funny Stories for Six Year Olds
Magical Stories for Six Year Olds
Animal Stories for Six Year Olds
Adventure Stories for Six Year Olds
Bedtime Stories for Six Year Olds

Funny Stories for Seven Year Olds
Magical Stories for Seven Year Olds
Animal Stories for Seven Year Olds
Adventure Stories for Seven Year Olds

Funny Stories for Eight Year Olds
Magical Stories for Eight Year Olds
Animal Stories for Eight Year Olds
Adventure Stories for Eight Year Olds

Funny Stories for Nine Year Olds
Magical Stories for Nine Year Olds
Animal Stories for Nine Year Olds
Adventure Stories for Nine Year Olds

Funny Stories for Ten Year Olds
Magical Stories for Ten Year Olds
Animal Stories for Ten Year Olds
Adventure Stories for Ten Year Olds

Coming soon

Revolting Stories for Nine Year Olds
Revolting Stories for Ten Year Olds

Adventure
STORIES
for Nine Year Olds

COMPILED BY HELEN PAIBA

ILLUSTRATED BY DOUGLAS CARREL

MACMILLAN
CHILDREN'S BOOKS

For Lior with love HP

First published 2001 by Macmillan Children's Books
a division of Macmillan Publishers Limited
25 Eccleston Place, London SW1W 9NF
Basingstoke and Oxford
www.macmillan.com

Associated companies throughout the world

ISBN 0 330 39141 0

3 5 7 9 8 6 4 2

A CIP catalogue record for this book is available from
the British Library.

Typeset by SX Composing DTP, Rayleigh, Essex
Printed and bound in Great Britain by
Mackays of Chatham plc, Kent

Contents

The Sad Knight

retold by Robert Leeson

Little John gazed up into the sky above the forest.

The sun rode high and bright. His eyes turned to the Trysting Tree, where Robin Hood leaned against the massive trunk, deep in thought. On the grass nearby sat Will Scarlet and Much the Miller's son. They glanced at one another, grinned and said nothing.

Then the noonday silence was broken by a sound like a rolling barrel. Little John's belly was rumbling. At last the big man spoke.

"Master! If we had dinner now, you'd be all the better for it."

Now Will and Much laughed. Robin shook his head.

"You know the rule, John. First we must have a guest, baron, abbot or knight, I don't care which, as long as he has the price of our meal in his pocket. Then when our guest is here, we shall say Mass, one for the Father, one for the Holy Ghost and one for our Dear Lady. And afterwards, we dine."

Little John looked up again at the sun. He spoke to himself, but everyone under the trees could hear him.

"The day's half gone. God send us a guest."

Robin smiled. "John, take your bow. Let Much and Will go with you. Walk up the Sayles as far as Watling Street. See who comes our way. You find a guest and I'll wager dinner will be ready when you come back."

Some little while later, the three outlaws stood upon the ridge above the Roman road. First they looked this way, then that. They could see a good mile in each direction. But no travellers came.

Little John's stomach growled again. The others began to chuckle, then stopped as they

Little John whispered in the leader's ear. "The knight's true enough. There's half a pound in his strong box and no more."

"Then serve more wine," called Robin, "and make it the best. The knight shall tell his story. No wonder you're dressed so poorly. Tell me, and be sure your secret shall be kept. Did they make you become a knight to get a fee from you?"

The outlaw chief looked shrewdly at the man's unhappy face. "Or have you lost your wealth in bad living, brawling and strife, lending and borrowing?"

The sad eyes flashed with temper for a moment.

"None of these, by God that made me. My father, his father before him for a hundred years and more, have been knights. Hear me, Robin Hood – a man may be in disgrace through no fault of his. It is God's will and God will put it right in the end."

"Tell your story, then."

More wine was poured. The outlaw band listened in silence as the knight spoke, his voice low.

7

"My name is Sir Richard of the Lee. Two years since, my neighbours could tell you, I earned well from my estates. But then I lost all. Only my family remains."

"Lost it? How?"

"Through folly and through kindness. My son, my heir, a fine boy, twenty years old, was a great champion on the tournament field. He killed a knight and a squire."

"To pay the price for this, and save him, I had to borrow four hundred pounds."

"Who did you borrow from?" asked Robin.

"From the rich Abbot of St Mary's."

"Ah, him."

"And now, the day to repay the money will soon be here. If I cannot find four hundred pounds, I will lose my castle, land and goods."

"If you cannot pay, what will you do?"

The knight's voice began to break. "I'll leave my own country and voyage to the Holy Land. I'll never return."

Sir Richard rose from table. "Farewell and thank you, Robin. There's no more to say."

Robin stood up. "Wait. Have you no friends to help you?"

"I had," answered the knight bitterly. "When I was rich, there were flocks of them. But now they run from me. They do not care to know me."

These last words brought tears to the eyes of the men in green who clustered round.

"So all you have is forfeit, just for four hundred pounds," said Robin. "Sir Richard, we shall lend you that. But who will guarantee your loan?"

The knight shrugged. "I have no name to offer, none but God in Heaven."

"Don't joke with me," Robin burst out. "God in Heaven? Why not St Peter or St Paul? Find some better guarantor, or get on the road again."

In despair, Sir Richard answered, "There is no other that I know, save our Dear Lady."

"Now we have it." Robin spoke with force. "I know of no better security in all England, than our Dear Lady."

He beckoned Little John.

"Go to our treasure chest. Count out twenty score pounds."

Little John did as he was bid. The gleaming

gold coins were scooped in great handfuls and thrown down on to his wide cloak where it lay on the grass.

"Count it properly," Much told him.

Little John glared back. "Hold your mouth, Much. This is to save a good knight from poverty."

Little John brought the money to table. Then he eyed the traveller.

"See the knight's clothes, Robin. We cannot let him go like that. You've got more cloth, scarlet and green, than any merchant in England."

"Measure Sir Richard three yards of each, then," came the reply.

Little John stood up once more and began to measure cloth, using his longbow as a yardstick. With each sweep of his great hand, he added three feet of Lincoln cloth.

Much stared. "What a devil's draper you are, John."

Will Scarlet joked, "John gives good measure, Much, because it costs him nothing."

Laughing, they brought the cloth to Sir

Richard and the men urged Robin, "Let him have a good horse, a grey courser, instead of that broken-down nag, and a saddle . . ."

Robin nodded. "And what will you give Sir Richard, Little John?"

"I'll give him a pair of shining gilt spurs, so he may think of our company and pray for us as he rides."

The knight mastered his feelings and spoke earnestly to Robin Hood. "When shall I repay you?"

"This day, twelve months from now, under this very tree," began Robin, then he paused in thought a while. "It is a shame for a knight to ride along, without a squire. Little John will ride with you and take a yeoman's place at your right hand.

"Now, Sir Richard, fare well, and God go with you. We meet in a year's time, on this spot."

In the cool gloom of his chamber sat the Abbot of St Mary's. This was a man who carried himself like a lord. His robes were grey but the cloth was rich.

Rings twinkled on his fingers as he picked up a parchment from the great oak table before him and read the script. Though faded with age, the writing was still clear. It pleased him.

There was a knock at the door and the Prior came in, slow and respectful. He had a gentle face, though his eyes were keen. And now they fell on the document in the Abbot's hands.

"Sir Richard's lands," he said.

The Abbot nodded. "Sir Richard's lands. This day twelve months ago he came to me and begged four hundred pounds in gold. And if he does not return with them today, he will lose all he owns."

Shaking his head, the Prior said, "It is a great pity a knight should lose his lands because he owes money."

He glanced at the window. "It is early yet. The day's not half gone. Perhaps he's on his way."

"Not he!" The Abbot spoke with force. "We shall see neither knight nor money. Good riddance."

12

The Prior raised his head to look the Abbot in the eye.

"You do him wrong. He may be over the sea, suffering hunger and cold, lying hard at night. If you take his lands it will be on your conscience."

"By God and St George!" burst out the Abbot. "Must you always be in my way?"

With these words the door opened again and the High Cellarer, a brawny monk with a huge head, entered.

"The knight is dead or hanged," he told the Abbot. "And the Abbey shall be four hundred pounds a year the better for it when we own his lands."

He bowed. "My lord, it is time to dine."

The Abbot rose and the others stood aside to let him pass. All three moved out into the arched passage and so to the Great Hall.

A lean, grey man, the Chief Justice, was waiting for them as they arrived at table. He eyed the scroll in the Abbot's hand.

"Sir Richard's deeds," said the Abbot. "If he does not bring four hundred pounds in gold today, he will be disinherited."

Casting a quick glance at the gleaming white cloth and rich spread of dishes, the justice answered, "He will not come. Let us dine."

The noonday sun shone on the city walls as a knight and his attendant, dressed gaily in red and green, rode through the gates. Their horses' hooves clattered over the cobbled streets and halted in front of the Abbey doors.

Sir Richard turned to the broad-shouldered man who rode behind him.

"Little John, before we enter, we'll change our clothes."

Quickly they dismounted and put on worn, travel-stained coats and mantles over their colourful tunics. As they were changing, the Abbey doors opened and the porter ran out, followed by stable boys. He bobbed his head to the knight.

"Welcome, good sir. My master has gone to dine. There are many gentlemen there, all waiting to see you."

His eye rested on the knight's grey courser

with its bright harness.

"That's a fine horse. Quick, lead it into the stables."

"No," said the knight sharply. "The horses stay outside. We shall not linger here."

He nodded to Little John and the two went into the Abbey.

The row of dark-robed men at table looked up from their eating in astonishment as the knight, dressed in dusty brown, and his tall servant marched into the hall.

Sir Richard advanced towards the table, but paused halfway and knelt down.

"Do gladly, my lord Abbot. I have kept my word and held to my day."

The Abbot did not return the greeting. "Have you brought the gold?" he asked.

Sir Richard's answer was just as short. "Not one penny."

Turning to the Chief Justice, the Abbot raised his wine cup. "There's a shameless debtor for you."

Then to the knight, he said, "Why are you here?"

"To beg you for more time to pay," answered

Sir Richard. Still on one knee, he appealed. "Sir Justice, be my friend. Protect me from those who would do me harm."

But the grey lawman only shook his head, his eyes shifting. "I owe the Abbot my loyalty. I owe him much else besides."

"Good sir Abbot," the knight tried once more. "If you will only hold my land for me while I get money to meet my debts, I will stay here and be your servant until you are paid."

Crash went the Abbot's fist upon the table. "By God you'll not get your land from me like that."

Anger filled Sir Richard at these harsh words. "By dear worthy God," he swore, "if I do not get back my lands, then someone will pay for it."

His eye swept over those at table. "A man should find out where his friends are before he is in need."

Now the Abbot stretched out an arm in fury. His look was full of loathing.

"False knight. Out from my hall and be quick."

Sir Richard leapt to his feet and replied

with equal strength.

"I'm no false knight and never have been. I've risked my life and limb in combat as readily as anyone. And as for you – to make a knight kneel for so long – you have no manners."

Leaning forward hastily, the Justice put in a word. "Can you not give the knight a sum of money to let his lands go? Otherwise you will never hold them in peace."

"A hundred pounds." The Abbot's voice was grudging.

"Say two hundred," urged the Justice.

"No, by God," broke in Sir Richard. "If you gave me a thousand pounds in gold, you will never be my heirs, Abbot, Justice or Monk."

Proudly, the knight strode to the table. Behind him the silent giant bore a great bag which clinked as they approached.

"Here's the gold you lent me," the knight told the Abbot. "Had you shown any courtesy, I would have paid you something extra for the loan."

Down fell the bag among the silver dishes. Now the Abbot had lost both appetite and tongue. But not for long. He rounded on the lawman.

"You can give me back the money I gave you."

"Not a penny, by God who died on the Tree," swore the Justice.

"Sir Abbot and men of law, I've held my day," the knight spoke in triumph. "Now I shall have my land again."

Reaching across the table, he plucked up the parchment scroll, turned on his heel and, with Little John close behind him, marched from the hall.

Outside in the sunshine, they stripped off the threadbare garb that covered their scarlet and green. Throwing the dusty clothes to the porter who stood by open-mouthed, they wheeled their horses about and galloped from the city.

As the sound of hooves in the distance reached her chamber, Sir Richard's lady wife ran down to the inner gate of the castle. Beyond the courtyard the portcullis was rising in the outer wall as the mounted party rode across in colourful array.

She greeted her husband as he leapt from his horse, asking him half in hope, half in fear, "Have you lost your lands, husband? Tell me!"

He shook his head and laughed.

"No, my lady. You must pray for Robin Hood. May his soul dwell in bliss for ever. He lent me money and his best man to ride at my side.

"I have dealt with the Abbot. He has his gold. We have our home and lands."

"But you must repay Robin Hood," she said.

"True," answered Sir Richard. "But now we have time on our side."

The Treasure Trove

Rob Marsh

This is a true story about an adventure that went wrong. I still think it was all Reggie's fault and he still blames me, but what we do agree on is that it all began the morning the two of us decided to bunk school for the day. This was not the sort of thing we usually did, though. Actually, neither of us had ever taken a day off school before. I suppose, the fact that the whole thing didn't turn out quite as we expected served us right. This may sound a bit unbelievable, but we both really like school so I'm not sure why we stayed away in the first place. Of course, everybody knows school is boring sometimes and there's always a test to be studied for, but the breaks are great: there's soccer in the winter and cricket in the summer so it's not as if it's all that bad! Anyway, I suppose I'm going off the point a bit so I'll slow down and go back to where I should have started all along – at the beginning.

I live three doors away from Reggie and the two of us walk to school together every day. It takes us twenty-five minutes, but if we're late, then we can do it in fifteen. Usually, we chat all the way and sometimes Reggie helps me with maths, because that's what he's really good at. Anyway, on the morning we found the treasure trove, I could tell Reggie was in a strange mood the moment I saw him. He had a serious look on his face and he didn't seem to want to talk much, which was quite unusual for him.

"What's bothering you?" I asked.

He just carried on walking, head down, staring at the pavement, as if he had the whole world resting on his shoulders.

"I don't want to go to school today," he answered miserably.

From the way he was acting I thought it might have been something serious.

"So, who does?" I said.

He shot an angry look at me. "No, I mean it. I'd like a day off."

I'd never actually considered bunking school until that moment, but the more I thought about it, the more I liked the idea.

"All right, why not?"

He looked at me as if he couldn't believe his ears were telling him the truth.

"Really?" he asked.

"Really," I answered.

Now that the decision to bunk school had been made, the next step was to decide where we were going to spend the day. Reggie's father worked in the Carlton Centre and although there wasn't much chance of us bumping into him, we decided to avoid the city centre completely. We caught a taxi that was going towards Observatory and fifteen minutes later we got out at a place called Bezuidenhout Park, which neither of us had ever been to before.

It was a beautiful spring day but most people were at work so there was hardly anyone about. I remember we told lots of jokes and pretended we were having a great time, but I think we both felt too guilty about taking the day off school to really enjoy ourselves. Actually, I'd had regrets even in the taxi and I suppose Reggie felt the same, though he didn't say so. We glanced at our watches. It was a little after 8.30 a.m., so school had already started. It was too late to go back so the only thing we could do was to try to make the best of it.

We strolled aimlessly along the pathways and eventually found ourselves in a remote corner of the park about as far away from the road as you could be. On a small hill there was a grove of trees and behind it there was a gully lined with thick bushes. The gully wasn't much more than a dent in the ground, but it was very secluded. We seemed to be the only people in the park, but I remember that as we headed down off the path a man was sitting on a bench reading a newspaper. Another man was walking his dog. Neither of them paid us the slightest bit of attention as we walked past.

When we got closer to the trees I noticed a

bit of silver paper glinting under one of the bushes. If the sun had been any higher in the sky, I don't think I would have noticed it. Something made me take a second look and that's when I saw there was a package of some kind hidden in the undergrowth.

I nudged Reggie. "What's that over there?" I said and went off to investigate.

He didn't know what I was talking about but he came to have a look anyway. The "package" turned out to be a cardboard apple-box, but it wasn't until I dragged it out into the open that I saw that whoever had put it under the bush had clearly made an effort to hide it. They'd even gone so far as to break off a few twigs and lay them on the top and around the sides as a kind of camouflage. When Reggie saw what I'd found, his eyes opened so wide they looked like enormous dinner-plates.

"Wow!" he said.

The box wasn't sealed so I pulled back the top flaps and we both peered inside. It was filled to the brim with chocolate bars, sweets, cigarettes and £50 notes! I gave a long, low whistle and Reggie, who was leaning over me, suddenly became breathless.

"It's a treasure trove!" he gasped.

I didn't answer, but I remember thinking that in all the books I'd ever read the main character would always bury the treasure and leave a map. It didn't seem right for treasure to be left, half-hidden under a bush in a cardboard box!

Reggie was also confused. "But why would anyone hide stuff like this?"

"Maybe they couldn't carry it and left it

here to go and get help?" I suggested, then felt stupid even before I'd finished the sentence.

"But what are we going to do with it?" Reggie asked anxiously.

I knew we had to take it to the police. That was the most sensible thing to do. Neither of us was in the habit of keeping things that didn't belong to us, but with a case full of chocolate bars and money staring at us, we had to get used to the idea first. After all, the police would just lock it up, say, "Thank you for being so honest, boys", and that would be the end of it.

Adventure over!

I was just about to say, "Let's carry it to the police station," when I heard a voice behind us.

"And what do you think you're doing?"

It was the man who I'd seen reading the newspaper. He was standing at the bottom of the bank, staring up at us with a really unpleasant smile on his face.

"What have you got there, boys?"

The second voice came from a man who'd been walking his dog. He was standing at the top of the bank struggling to hold back the animal which was glaring at us, its nose wrinkling back each time it growled. I don't know how they'd managed to sneak up on us without us realizing it, but at that moment we were hemmed in and I had an uncomfortable feeling that our fortunes had taken a distinct turn for the worst.

"So we've finally caught the little thieves," the first one said.

"Little thieves?" I thought, then the realization dawned on me. Reggie and I looked at each other in disbelief. Obviously, the whole thing was just an unfortunate misunderstanding which we'd be able to clear up in no time at all.

I spoke to the one at the bottom of the bank.

"I think you've made a mistake, sir," I began.

The man's smile widened. "Oh, we've made a mistake have we? And what mistake is that?"

"We've just found these, sir," Reggie said.

The other policeman said, "Oh, I see,"

making us turn around and look up at him. "You were on your way to school, just happened to take a diversion into the park, came across a box of stolen goods and just happened to be about to take them to the station when we came on the scene?"

His voice was heavy with sarcasm and I didn't like the way he kept saying "happened".

We nodded. "Yes, that's exactly it," I said.

They both laughed and the dog showed its fangs again, but somehow I don't think it was laughing. I knew then that things didn't look good for us at all.

"That's the truth. Honestly," I said weakly.

"Your school starts late, doesn't it?" the first one asked coldly.

That was a difficult one. I heard Reggie swallow and that's when I wished I could disappear into thin air. We were guilty until proven innocent to these men, it seemed.

"These two young scholars are clearly exemplary pupils, George," he said, smirking. He was being sarcastic again.

"We were just going to bring this lot to the

police," Reggie repeated, but I knew it was no use.

"Were you?"

Before we had a chance to answer he clambered up the bank and grabbed us both quite roughly by the arms.

"I think we'll continue this conversation back at the Main Road police station, Lucas," he said.

It was then that I panicked.

"But what about the goods?" I said.

"We'll bring the package along with us,

won't we?" he answered and then let go of my arm so I could pick up the box to carry it with me.

I saw my chance. That's when I made a run for it. I gave him a swift dig in the ribs, heard him grunt with pain, and ducked under his flailing arm. I sprinted down the bank before he had time to recover. "Ooh! You little devil!" he wheezed.

A little while later I turned and looked back at them. Neither of the policemen had made the slightest effort to chase me, though they'd both got hold of Reggie's arms. They were simply standing at the bottom of the bank staring at me. Then it dawned on me. Why should they be concerned at all about me? They'd got Reggie and they'd seen the school uniforms we were wearing. It wouldn't take a genius to track us down, even if we both escaped.

"It's no use running off," the one shouted. "Your friend won't be going anywhere."

He gave Reggie a shake just to emphasize the point, then the three of them marched off towards the road. I followed at a distance, but it wasn't until I'd watched them drive away that I realized the seriousness of the situation.

Not only could we be charged for theft, but to make matters worse, I'd struck a police officer and escaped from custody. I'd woken up as an ordinary person and was now a criminal on the run! Things looked bleak. The only way I could prove our innocence was to find the guilty party and bring him or her to justice. But how was I supposed to do that? It seemed I had only one alternative: I would have to stake out the site and hope that whoever had hidden the parcel under the bush returned to collect it.

Then I could get a car registration number or a description of the thief.

It was a small chance, but it was all I had. I managed to find a good spot from which I could keep an eye on the place where the box had been hidden. I took out a geography book and sat down to study. Without a doubt that was the longest morning of my life. I read the same chapter at least twenty-five times! I just couldn't concentrate. I kept imagining Reggie being interrogated by the police and then getting thrown into a damp and dark cell with drug dealers and pickpockets and hit-men. That's the fate which I also imagined awaited me, after I'd brought disgrace and disaster on my family. I finally knew what it felt like to be a wanted man. It wasn't pleasant.

It was just before twelve when I spotted the man I'd been waiting for. The moment I saw him it occurred to me he was just too suspicious-looking to be anything else but a criminal. He was small and shrivelled-looking with thinning black hair. He was wearing a heavy overcoat that was at least two sizes too big for him. He shuffled along with his hands in his pockets and his shoulders were hunched over. Every so often he would stop and look around to see if anyone was looking at him. It was so obvious what he was doing I might have laughed if I hadn't been so scared.

Before he got to the place where the box had been hidden he paused and lit a cigarette.

He looked around again and I felt his eyes pass over me. My head was bearing down into *Dairy Cattle and Sheep* so I don't think he took any notice of me. When I looked up again he was kneeling down in front of the bush, pushing back the branches. Even from where I was sitting I could see the anger in his face when he stood up again. I saw him throw his cigarette on to the ground with all the force he could muster and then he headed back towards the road. I closed my textbook casually, put it in my bag and set off after him.

The man never once looked back to see if he was being followed. He headed out of the park and ten minutes later we were in a part of the city where the streets were narrow and the pavements crowded with hawkers. Because of the rush of midday shoppers, it was quite difficult to keep him in sight without making myself too visible.

Suddenly, he slipped down an alleyway to the place where it opened into another busy street, but he seemed to have vanished into thin air. That was when I really started to panic. I remember saying, "Oh, please, don't let this happen to me," as I ran anxiously up and down the road. When I got back to the alleyway I didn't know what to do and it was just out of sheer luck that I happened to overhear raised voices coming from the other side of a wall nearby.

"I'm telling you it was gone, Jack. I would not have left it there last night if I hadn't seen the police car. Now somebody's robbed us!"

The reply when it came wasn't loud enough for me to make out, but there was no mistaking the tone of outrage in the voice. That was when I knew I'd found the thieves. But somehow, I just had to get some more evidence.

I pressed my ear against the backyard gate, but the men suddenly dropped their voices to a whisper so I couldn't hear a thing they said. I did hear them walk away towards a building, though.

The latch worked as smoothly as silk when I tried it. I opened the gate a fraction and pressed an eye to the opening. In the centre of a cluttered scrapyard I could see the rustling hulk of a motorcar propped up on bricks and beyond it a warehouse of some kind. There was a door open at the back of the building and I could hear some people moving around inside.

I took a deep breath, slipped into the yard and hid behind an old fridge.

With my heart beating like a drum, I crept around the wall, slowly making my way to the open doorway. Summoning my courage, I peeped into the building. Inside the warehouse a group of men were loading boxes on to a lorry but the man I had followed and the one named Jack, were in a glassed-in office off to one side. Jack was lying back in an office chair with his feet on the desk, while the other man was pacing the floor. They were still arguing about the missing box. I knew I had to find a way to eavesdrop.

I noticed an open skylight high up in the wall behind the desk Jack was sitting at. I began to think of a plan. I was so scared I almost couldn't breathe properly. I sneaked around the side of the building. Between the warehouse and a wall was a narrow alleyway.

When I stood panting beneath the window outside Jack's office, all I could hear was a murmur of voices. I just had to get higher.

It was then that I noticed the empty dustbin nearby. Great! I thought that sort of good luck only happened in the movies. But there it was, just waiting to be used. Quietly, I dragged it underneath the window and then carefully climbed on top. Believe me, trying to clamber up on to a dustbin and keeping quiet at the same time is not as easy as it sounds! Balancing somehow, I could just about see over the bottom ledge of the window. Jack and the other man were still having a heated conversation.

"If I ever find out who pinched that box I'll skin them alive," the man I'd followed was saying. Jack suddenly started to laugh, jerking and hissing with the effort.

"So, what's so funny about that?" the other one asked sharply.

"Maybe we should claim on theft insurance?" Jack suggested. "Although I'm not sure if having stolen goods stolen constitutes crime."

His companion was not amused. "In my book, losing £2,000 is no laughing matter. Let me remind you, Jack. Breaking into that supermarket was no picnic," he said angrily.

I was standing on tip-toe and tried to shift my weight a little. That's when I lost my balance. I hit the ground at the same time as the bin, which tipped over with a loud clatter but I was up and running even before the lid had stopped rolling. I knew I couldn't make it out the back door again so the only alternative was to jump over the wall behind me. I tossed my bag over, walked back a few paces, ran and grabbed hold of the top of the wall and flipped myself over in three seconds flat. I landed in a vegetable patch. Quickly, I hid amongst the tomatoes. I heard footsteps run along the building on the far side of the wall and then there was the sound of the bin being righted.

"Damn cats!" somebody muttered. A couple of other men came around the side also to see what the commotion was all about. They soon went away again. Phew, that had been a very close call! After that I sidled down the side of the house and came out into the street again. I headed for the police station.

Half an hour later I was ushered into Lucas's office. Reggie and the detectives looked at me as if they'd just seen a ghost. It was not at all the scene I was expecting: Reggie was sipping a cup of tea and eating a sandwich and the three of them seemed to be chatting away like old friends. Noticing my agitated manner, the detective named Lucas asked me what the matter was.

I was almost completely out of breath but managed to blurt out, "I know who the real thieves are!" For a second, the two detectives looked at each other.

"What do you mean you know who the thieves are?" they both asked.

"I waited in the park and then when someone came looking for the parcel I followed him. The man I followed is thin and he's wearing a big overcoat. He went to a warehouse where some other men were loading stolen goods on to a lorry. A man named Jack is his partner. I can take you there but we must hurry, I don't know for how

long they are going to be there." The two
detectives didn't need further urging. One of
them got on the phone and the other went off
to see the Head of Detectives.

A minute later we were all hurrying down
the stairs to a car park at the back of the
police station where three cars were waiting
with their engines running. We all got in the
leading vehicle as the other two were already
filled with policemen, and screeched out of
the yard.

The capture was a bit of an anti-climax
really. One car dropped some policemen
around the back of the warehouse, while the
rest of us pulled up at the front.

At a signal from George everybody rushed
inside and in a few seconds it was all over.
The thieves were caught red-handed as they
were completely unprepared. They gave
themselves up without a fight.

George later formally thanked us for the
help we'd given the police and offered to send
us home in a police car but in the end we
decided to use a taxi. I'm sure we would have
got our pictures in the paper and probably a

reward as well, but we'd bunked school and the last thing we wanted to do was tell the world about it. Of course, we should have told our parents. In fact, they never did find out, but that would have caused a whole new set of problems. So, in the end, we just kept quiet about the whole thing. After all, we'd learnt our lesson. There didn't seem much point to add insult to injury.

Reggie and I haven't bunked school since and I'm quite certain we never will. Sometimes we joke about it. I still think we were lucky we didn't get into bigger trouble, but we did have an adventure so maybe the day wasn't a total disaster, after all . . .

The Dark Streets of Kimball's Green

Joan Aiken

"**E**m! You, Em! Where has that dratted child got to? Em! Wait till I lay hold of you, I won't half tan you!"

Mrs Bella Vaughan looked furiously up and down the short street. She was a stocky woman, with short, thick, straight grey hair, parted on one side and clamped back by a grip; a cigarette always dangled from one corner of her mouth and, as soon as it dwindled down, another grew there. "Em! Where have you got to?" she yelled again.

"Here I am, Mrs Vaughan!" Emmeline dashed anxiously round the corner.

"Took long enough about it! The Welfare

Lady's here, wants to know how you're getting on. Here, let's tidy you up."

Mrs Vaughan pulled a comb and handkerchief out of her tight-stretched apron pocket, dragged the comb sharply through Emmeline's hair, damped the handkerchief with spit and scrubbed it over Emmeline's flinching face.

"Hello, Emmeline. Been out playing?" said the Welfare Lady, indoors. "That's right. Fresh air's the best thing for them, isn't it, Mrs Vaughan?"

"She's always out," grunted Mrs Vaughan. "Morning, noon and night. I don't hold with kids frowsting about indoors. Not much traffic round here."

"Well, Emmeline, how are you getting on? Settling down with Mrs Vaughan, quite happy, are you?"

Emmeline looked at her feet and muttered something. She was thin and small for her age, dark-haired and pale-cheeked.

"She's a mopey kid," Mrs Vaughan pronounced. "Always want to be reading, if I didn't tell her to run out of doors."

"Fond of reading, are you?" the Welfare Lady said kindly. "And what do you read, then?"

"Books," muttered Emmeline. The Welfare Lady's glance strayed to the huge, untidy pile of magazines on the telly.

"Kid'll read anything she could lay hands on, if I let her," Mrs Vaughan said. "I don't though. What good does reading do you? None that I know of."

"Well, I'm glad you're getting on all right, Emmeline. Be a good girl and do what Mrs Vaughan tells you. And I'll see you next month again." She got into her tiny car and drove off to the next of her endless list of calls.

"Right," said Mrs Vaughan. "I'm off too, down to the town hall to play bingo. So you hop it, and mind you're here on the doorstep at eleven sharp or I'll skin you."

Emmeline murmured something.

"Stay indoors? Not on your nelly! And have them saying, if the house burnt down, that I oughtn't to have left you on your own?"

"It's so cold out." A chilly September wind

scuffled the bits of paper in the street. Emmeline shivered in her thin coat.

"Well, run about then, and keep warm! Fresh air's good for you, like that interfering old busybody said. Anyway she's come and gone for the month, that's something. Go on, hop it now."

So Emmeline hopped it.

Kimball's Green where Mrs Vaughan had her home, was a curious, desolate little corner of London. It lay round the top of a hill, which was crowned with a crumbling, blackened church, St Chad's. The four or five streets of tiny, aged houses were also crumbling and blackened, all due for demolition and most of them empty. The houses were so old that they seemed shrunk and wrinkled, like old apples or old faces, and they were immeasurably, unbelievably dirty, with the dirt of hundreds of years. Around the little hill was a flat, desolate tract of land, Wansea Marches, which nobody had even tried to use until the nineteenth century; then it became covered with railway goods yards and brick-works and gas-works and an electric power station, all of which belched their black smoke over the little island of Kimball's Green on the hilltop.

You could hardly think anybody would *choose* to live in such a cut-off part, but Mrs Vaughan had been born in Sylvan Street, near the top of the hill, and she declared she wasn't going to shift until they came after her with a bulldozer. She took in foster children when they grew too old for the Wansea Orphanage, and, though it wasn't a very healthy neighbourhood, what with the smoke and the damp from the marshes, there were so many orphans, and so few homes for them to go to, that Emmeline was the latest of a large number who had stayed with Mrs Vaughan. But there were very few other children in the district now; very few inhabitants at all, except old and queer ones who camped secretly in the condemned houses. Most people found it too far to go to the shops: an eighty-penny bus ride, all the way past the goods yards and the gas-works, to Wansea High Street.

So far as anyone knew, Emmeline belonged

in the neighbourhood; she had been found on the step of St Chad's one windy March night; but in spite of this, or because of it, she was rather frightened by the nest of little dark empty streets. She was frightened by many things, among which were Mrs Vaughan and her son Colin. And she particularly hated the nights, five out of seven, when Mrs Vaughan went off to play bingo, leaving Emmeline outside in the street. Indeed, if it hadn't been for two friends, Emmeline really didn't know how she could have borne those evenings.

As Mrs Vaughan's clumping steps died away down the hill, one of the friends appeared: his thin form twined out from between some old black railings and he rubbed encouragingly against Emmeline's ankles, sticking up his tail in welcome.

"Oh, Scrawny! there you are," she said with relief. "Here, I've saved you a piece of cheese-rind from tea."

Old Scrawny was a tattered, battered tabby, with ragged whiskers, crumpled ears, and much fur missing from his tail; he had no owner and lived on what he could find; he ate the cheese-rind with a lot of loud, vulgar, guzzling noise, and hardly washed at all afterwards; but Emmeline loved him dearly, and he loved her back. Every night she left her window open and old Scrawny climbed in, by various gutters, drain-pipes, and the wash-house roof. Mrs Vaughan wouldn't have allowed such a thing for a minute if she had known, but Emmeline always took care that old Scrawny had left long before she was called in the morning.

When the rind was finished Scrawny jumped into Emmeline's arms and she tucked her hands for warmth under his scanty fur; they went up to the end of the street by the church, where there was a telephone box. Like the houses around it was old and dirty, and it had been out of order for so many years that now nobody even bothered to thump its box for coins. The only person who used it was Emmeline, and she used it almost every night, unless gangs were roaming the streets and throwing stones, in which case she hid behind a dustbin or under a flight of area steps. But when the gangs had gone elsewhere the call-box made a very convenient shelter; best of all, it was even light enough to read there, because although the bulb in the call-box had been broken long ago, a street lamp shone right overhead.

"No book tonight, Scrawny, unless Mr Yakkymo comes and brings me another," said Emmeline, "so what shall we do? Shall we phone somebody, or shall I tell you a story?"

Scrawny purred, dangling round her neck like a striped scarf.

"We'll ring somebody up, shall we? All right."

She let the heavy door close behind her. Inside it was not exactly warm, but at least they were out of the wind. Scrawny climbed from Emmeline's shoulder into the compartment where the telephone books would have been if somebody hadn't made off with them; Emmeline picked up the broken receiver and dialled.

"Hello, can I speak to King Cunobel? Hello, King Cunobel, I am calling to warn you. A great army is approaching your fort – the Tribe of the Children of Darkness. Under

their wicked queen Belavaun they are coming to attack your stronghold with spears and chariots. You must tell your men to be extra brave; each man must arm himself with his bow and a sheaf of arrows, two spears and a sword. Each man must have his faithful wolfhound by his side." She stroked old Scrawny, who seemed to be listening intently. "Your men are far outnumbered by the Children of Dark, King Cunobel, so you must tell your Chief Druid to prepare a magic drink, made from vetch and mallow and succory, to give them courage. The leaves must be steeped in mud and left to gather dew for two nights, until you have enough to wet each man's tongue. Then they will be brave enough to beat off the Children of Dark and save your camp."

She listened for a moment or two with her ear pressed against the silent receiver, and then said to old Scrawny,

"King Cunobel wants to know what will happen if the Children of Dark get to the fort before the magic drink is prepared?"

"Morow," said Scrawny. He jumped down

from the bookshelf and settled himself on Emmeline's feet, where there was more room to stretch out.

"My faithful wolfhound says you must order your men to make high barricades of brambles and thorns," Emmeline told King Cunobel. "Build them in three rings round the encampment, and place one-third of your men inside each ring. King Cunobel and the Druids will be in the middle ring. Each party must fight to the death in order to delay the Children of Dark until the magic drink is ready. Do you understand? Then goodbye and good luck."

She listened again.

"He wants to know who *I* am," she told Scrawny, and she said into the telephone, "I am a friend, the Lady Emmeline, advised by her faithful enchanted wolfhound Catuscraun. I wish you well."

Then she rang off and said to Scrawny, "Do you think I had better call the Chief Druid and tell him to hurry up with that magic drink?"

Old Scrawny shut his eyes.

"No," she agreed, "you're right, it would only distract him. I know, I'll ring up the wicked Queen of Dark."

She dialled again and said:

"Hello, is that the wicked Queen Belavaun? This is your greatest enemy, ringing up to tell you that you will never, never capture the stronghold of King Cunobel. Not if you besiege it for three thousand years! King Cunobel has a strong magic that will defeat you. All your tribes, the Trinovans and the Votadins and the Damnons and the Bingonii will be eaten by wolves and wild boars. Not a man will remain! And you will lose all your wealth and power and your purple robes and fur cloaks, you will have nothing left but a miserable old mud cabin outside King Cunobel's stronghold, and every day his men will look over the walls and laugh at you. Goodbye, and bad luck to you for ever!"

She rang off and said to Scrawny, "That frightened her."

Scrawny was nine-tenths asleep, but at this moment footsteps coming along the street made him open his eyes warily. Emmeline was alert too. The call-box made a good look-out point, but it would be a dangerous place in which to be trapped.

"It's all right," she said to Scrawny, then. "It's only Mr Yakkymo."

She opened the door and they went to meet their other friend.

Mr Yakkymo (he spelt his name Iachimo, but Yakkymo was the way it sounded) came limping slightly up the street until he reached them; then he rubbed the head of old Scrawny (who stuck his tail up) and handed Emmeline a book. It was old and small, with a mottled binding and gilt-edged leaves; it was called *The Ancient History of Kimball's Green and Wansea Marshes*, and it came from Wansea Borough Library.

Emmeline's eyes opened wide with delight. She began reading the book at once, skipping from page to page.

"Why, this tells all about King Cunobel! It's even better than the one you brought about ancient London. Have you read this, Mr Yakkymo?"

He nodded, smiling. He was a thin, bent old

man with rather long white hair; as well as the book he carried a leather case, which contained a flute, and when he was not speaking he would often open this case and run his fingers absently up and down the instrument.

"I thought you would find it of interest," he said. "It's a pity Mrs Vaughan won't let you go to the public library yourself."

"She says reading only puts useless stuck-up notions in people's heads," Emmeline said dreamily, her eyes darting up and down the pages of the book. "Listen! It tells what King Cunobel wore – a short kilt with a gold belt. His chest was painted blue with woad, and he had a gold collar round his neck and a white cloak with gold embroidery. He carried a shield of beaten brass and a short sword. On his head he wore a fillet of gold, and on his arm gold armlets. His house was built of mud and stone, with a thatched roof; the walls were hung with skins and the floor strewn with rushes."

They had turned and were walking slowly along the street; old Scrawny, after the

manner of cats, sometimes loitered behind investigating doorsteps and dark crannies, sometimes darted ahead and then waited for them to come up with him.

"Do you think any of King Cunobel's descendants still live here?" Emmeline said.

"It is just possible."

"Tell me some more about what it was like here then."

"All the marshes – the part where the brick-works and the goods yards are now – would have been covered by forest and threaded by slow-flowing streams."

"Threaded by slow-flowing streams," Emmeline murmured to herself.

"All this part would be Cunobel's village. Little mud huts, each with a door and a chimney hole, thatched with reeds."

Emmeline looked at the pavements and rows of houses, trying to imagine them away, trying to imagine forest trees and little thatched huts.

"There would be a stockade of logs and thorns all round. A bigger hall for the king, and one for the Druids near the sacred grove."

"Where was that?"

"Up at the top of the hill, probably. With a specially sacred oak in the middle. There is an oak tree, still, in St Chad's churchyard; maybe it's sprung from an acorn of the Druid's oak."

"Maybe it's the same one? Oaks live a long time, don't they?"

"Hark!" he said checking. "What's that?"

The three of them were by the churchyard wall; they kept still and listened. Next moment they all acted independently, with the speed of long practice: Mr Iachimo, murmuring, "Good night, my child," slipped away round a corner; Emmeline wrapped her precious book in a polythene bag and poked it into a hole in the wall behind a loose stone; then she and old Scrawny raced downhill, back to Mrs Vaughan's house. She crouched panting on the doorstep, old Scrawny leapt up on to a shed roof and out of reach, just as a group of half a dozen people came swaggering and singing along the street.

"What was that?" one of them called.

"A cat."

"Let's go after it!"

"No good. It's gone."

When they got to Mrs Vaughan's their chief left the others and came over to Emmeline.

"It's you, is it, Misery?" he said. "Where's Ma?"

"Out at bingo."

"She would be. I wanted to get a bit of the old girl's pension off her before she spent it all."

He gave Emmeline's hair a yank and flipped her nose, hard and painfully, with his thumbnail. She looked at him in stony silence, biting her lip.

"Who's *she*, Col?" a new gang-member asked. "Shall we chivvy her?"

"She's one of my ma's orphanage brats – just a little drip. Ma won't let me tease her, so long as she's indoors, or on the step. But watch it, you, if we catch you in the street." Colin flipped Emmeline's nose again and they drifted off, kicking at anything that lay on the pavement.

At half-past eleven Mrs Vaughan came home from her bingo and let in the shivering Emmeline, who went silently up to her bed in the attic. At eleven thirty-five old Scrawny jumped with equal silence on to her stomach, and the two friends curled round each other for warmth.

Colin was not at breakfast next morning. Often he spent nights on end away from home; his mother never bothered to ask where.

Emmeline had to run errands and do housework in the morning but in the afternoon Mrs Vaughan, who wanted a nap, told her to clear off and not show her face a minute before six. That gave her five whole hours for reading; she dragged on her old coat and flew up to the churchyard.

The door in the high black wall was always kept locked, but somebody had once left a lot of rusty old metal pipes stacked in an angle of the wall; Emmeline, who weighed very little more than old Scrawny, clambered carefully up them, and so over.

Inside, the churchyard was completely overgrown. Blackthorn, plane and sycamore trees were entangled with great clumps of bramble. Groves of mares'-tails, chin-high to Emmeline, covered every foot of the ground. It made a perfect place to come and hide by day, but was too dark at night and too full of pitfalls; pillars and stone slabs leaned every which way, hidden in the vegetation.

Emmeline flung herself down on the flat tomb of Admiral Sir Horace Tullesley Campbell and read her book; for three hours she never moved; then she closed it with a sigh, so as to leave some for the evening in case Mrs Vaughan went out.

A woodpecker burst yammering from the tallest tree as Emmeline shut the book. Could that be the Druid's oak, she wondered, and started to push her way through to it. Brambles scratched her face and tore her clothes; Mrs Vaughan would punish her but that couldn't be helped. And at last she was there. The tree stood in a little clear space of bare leaf-mould. It was an oak, a big one, with a gnarled, massive trunk and roots like knuckles thrusting out of the ground. This made an even better secret place for reading than the Admiral's tomb, and Emmeline wished once again that it wasn't too dark to read in the churchyard at night.

St Chad's big clock said a quarter to six, so she left *The Ancient History of Kimball's Green* in its plastic bag hidden in a hollow of the tree and went draggingly home; then realized, too late, that her book would be exceedingly hard to find once dark had fallen.

Mrs Vaughan, who had not yet spent all her week's money, went out to bingo again that evening, so Emmeline returned to the telephone box and rang up King Cunobel.

"Is that the King? I have to tell you that your enemies are five miles nearer. Queen Belavaun is driving a chariot with scythes on its wheels, and her wicked son Coluon leads a band of savage followers; he carries a sling and a gold-handled javelin and is more cruel than any of the band. Has the Chief Druid prepared the magic drink yet?"

She listened and old Scrawny, who as usual was sitting at her feet, said "Prtnrow?"

"The Chief Druid says they have made the drink, Scrawny, and put it in a flagon of beaten bronze, which has been set beneath the sacred oak until it is needed. Meanwhile the warriors are feasting on wheat-cakes, boars' flesh and mead."

Next she rang up Queen Belavaun and hissed, "Oh wicked queen, your enemies are massing against you! You think that you will triumph, but you are wrong! Your son will be taken prisoner, and you will be turned out of your kingdom; you will be forced to take refuge with the Iceni or the Brigantes."

It was still only half-past nine, and Mr Iachimo probably would not come this evening, for two nights out of three he went to play his flute outside a theatre in the West End of London.

"Long ago I was a famous player and people came from all over Europe to hear me," he had told Emmeline sadly, one wet evening when they were sheltering together in the church porch.

"What happened? Why aren't you famous now?"

"I took to drink," he said mournfully. "Drink gives you hiccups. You can't play the flute with hiccups."

"You don't seem to have hiccups now."

"Now I can't afford to drink any longer."

"So you can play the flute again," Emmeline said triumphantly.

"True," he agreed; he pulled out his instrument and blew a sudden dazzling shower of notes into the rainy dark. "But now it is too late. Nobody listens; nobody remembers the name of Iachimo. And I have grown too old and tired to make them remember."

"Poor Mr Yakkymo," Emmeline thought, recalling this conversation. "*He* could do with a drop of King Cunobel's magic drink; then he'd be able to make people listen to him."

She craned out of the telephone box to look at St Chad's clock: quarter to ten. The streets were quiet tonight; Colin's gang had got money from somewhere and were down at the Wansea Palais.

"I'm going to get my book," Emmeline suddenly decided. "At least I'm going to try. There's a moon, it shouldn't be too dark to see. Coming, Scrawny?"

Scrawny intimated, stretching, that he didn't mind.

The churchyard was even stranger under the moon than by daylight; the mares'-tails threw their zebra-striped shadows everywhere and an owl flew hooting across the path; old Scrawny yakkered after it indignantly to come back and fight fair, but the owl didn't take up his challenge.

"I don't suppose it's really an owl," Emmeline whispered. "Probably one of Queen Belavaun's spies. We must make haste."

Finding the oak tree was not so hard as she had feared, but finding the book was a good deal harder, because under the tree's thick leaves and massive branches no light could penetrate; Emmeline groped and fumbled among the roots until she was quite sure she must have been right round the tree at least three times. At last her right hand slipped into a deep crack; she rummaged about hopefully, her fingers closed on something, but what she pulled out was a small round object, tapered at one end. She stuck it in her coat pocket and went on searching. "The book must be somewhere, Scrawny; unless Queen Belavaun's spy has stolen it."

At last she found it; tucked away where she could have sworn she had searched a dozen times already.

"Thank goodness! Now we'd better hurry, or there won't be any time for reading after all."

Emmeline was not sorry to leave the churchyard behind; it felt *crowded*, as if King Cunobel's warriors were hiding there, shoulder to shoulder among the bushes, keeping vigilant watch; Sylvan Street outside was empty and lonely in comparison. She scurried into the phone box, clutching Scrawny against her chest.

"Now listen while I read to you about the Druids, Scrawny: they wore long white robes and they liked mistletoe – there's some mistletoe growing on that oak tree, I'm positive! – and they used rings of sacred stones too. Maybe some of the stones in the churchyard are left over from the Druids."

Scrawny purred agreeingly, and Emmeline looked up the hill, trying to move St Chad's church out of the way and replace it by a grove of sacred trees with aged, white-robed men among them.

Soon it was eleven o'clock: time to hide the book behind the stone and wait for Mrs Vaughan on the doorstep. Along with his mother came Colin, slouching and bad-tempered.

"Your face is all scratched," he told Emmeline. "You look a sight."

"What have you been up to?" Mrs Vaughan said sharply.

Emmeline was silent but Colin said, "Reckon it's that mangy old cat she's always lugging about."

"Don't let me see you with a cat round *this* house," Mrs Vaughan snapped. "Dirty, sneaking things, never know where they've been. If any cat comes in here, I tell you, I'll get Colin to wring its neck!"

Colin smiled; Emmeline's heart turned right over with horror. But she said nothing and crept off upstairs to bed; only, when Scrawny arrived later, rather wet because it had begun to rain, she clutched him convulsively tight; a few tears wouldn't make much difference to the dampness of his fur.

"Humph!" said Mrs Vaughan, arriving early and unexpectedly in Emmeline's attic. "I thought as much!"

She leaned to slam the window but Scrawny, though startled out of sleep, could still move ten times faster than any human; he was out and over the roof in a flash.

"Look at that!" said Mrs Vaughan. "Filthy, muddy cat's footprints all over my blankets!

Well that's one job you'll do this morning, my young madam – you'll wash those blankets. And you'll have to sleep without blankets till they're dried – I'm not giving you any other. Daresay they're all full of fleas' eggs too."

Emmeline, breakfastless, crouched over the tub in the back wash-house; she did not much mind the job, but her brain was giddy with worry about Scrawny; how could she protect him? Suppose he were to wait for her, as he sometimes did, outside the house. Mrs Vaughan had declared that she would go after him with the chopper if she set eyes on him; Colin had sworn to hunt him down.

"All right, hop it now," Mrs Vaughan said, when the blankets satisfied her. "Clear out, don't let me see you again before six. No dinner? Well, I can't help that, can I? You should have finished the washing by dinner-time. Oh, all right, here's a bit of bread and marge, now make yourself scarce. I can't abide kids about the house all day."

Emmeline spent most of the afternoon in a vain hunt for Scrawny. Perhaps he had retired to some hidey-hole for a nap, as he often did at that time of day; but perhaps Colin had caught him already?

"Scrawny, Scrawny," she called softly and despairingly at the mouths of alleys, outside gates, under trees and walls; there was no reply. She went up to the churchyard, but a needle in a hundred haystacks would be easier to find than Scrawny in that wilderness if he did not choose to wake and show himself.

Giving up for the moment Emmeline went in search of Mr Iachimo, but he was not to be found either; he had never told Emmeline where he lived and was seldom seen by daylight; she thought he probably inhabited one of the condemned houses and was ashamed of it.

It was very cold; a grey, windy afternoon turning gloomily to dusk. Emmeline pushed cold hands deep in her pockets; her fingers met and explored a round, unusual object. Then she remembered the thing she had picked up in the dark under the oak tree. She pulled it out, and found she was holding a tiny flask, made of some dark lustreless metal tarnished with age and crusted with earth. It was not quite empty; when Emmeline shook it she could hear liquid splashing about inside, but very little, not more than a few drops.

"Why," she breathed, just for a moment forgetting her fear in the excitement of this discovery, "it is – it *must* be the Druids' magic drink! But why, why didn't the warriors drink it?"

She tried to get out the stopper; it was made of some hard blackish substance, wood, or leather that had become hard as wood in the course of years.

"Can I help you, my child?" said a gentle voice above her head.

Emmeline nearly jumped out of her skin – but it was only Mr Iachimo, who had hobbled silently up the street.

"Look – look, Mr Yakkymo! Look what I found under the big oak in the churchyard! It must be the Druids' magic drink – mustn't it? Made of mallow and vetch and succory, steeped in mead, to give warriors courage. It must be!"

He smiled at her; his face very kind. "Yes, indeed it must!" he said.

But somehow, although he was agreeing with her, for a moment Emmeline had a twinge of queer dread, as if there was nothing – nothing at all – left in the world to hold on to; as if even Mr Iachimo were not what he seemed but, perhaps, a spy sent by Queen Belavaun to steal the magic flagon.

Then she pushed down her fear, taking a deep breath, and said, "Can you get the stopper out, Mr Yakkymo?"

"I can try," he said, and brought out a tiny foreign-looking penknife shaped like a fish with which he began prising the fossil-hard black substance in the neck of the bottle. At last it began to crumble.

"Take care – do take care," Emmeline said. "There's only a very little left. Perhaps the defenders did drink most of it. But anyway there's enough left for you, Mr Yakkymo."

"For me, my child? Why for me?"

"Because you need to be made brave so that you can make people listen to you play your flute."

"Very true," he said thoughtfully. "But do not you need bravery too?"

Emmeline's face clouded. "What good would bravery do me?" she said. "*I'm* all right – it's old Scrawny I'm worried about. Oh, Mr Yakkymo, Colin and Mrs Vaughan say they are going to *kill* Scrawny. What can I do?"

"You must tell them they have no right to."

"*That* wouldn't do any good," Emmeline said miserably. "Oh! – You've got it out!"

The stopper had come out, but it had also crumbled away entirely.

"Never mind," Emmeline said. "You can put in a bit of the cotton wool that you use to clean your flute. What does it smell of, Mr Yakkymo?"

His face had changed as he sniffed; he looked at her oddly. "Honey and flowers," he said.

Emmeline sniffed too. There was a faint – very faint – aromatic, sweet fragrance.

"Wet your finger, Mr Yakkymo, and lick it! Please do! It'll help you, I know it will!"

"Shall I?"

"Yes, do, do!"

He placed his finger across the opening, and quickly turned the bottle upside down and back, then looked at his fingertip. There was the faintest drop of moisture on it.

"Quick – don't waste it," Emmeline said, breathless with anxiety.

He licked his finger.

"Well, does it taste?"

"No taste." But he smiled, and bringing out a wad of cotton tissue, stuffed a piece of it into the mouth of the flask, which he handed to Emmeline.

"This is yours, my child. Guard it well! Now, as to your friend Scrawny – I will go and see Mrs Vaughan tomorrow, if you can protect him until then."

"Thank you!" she said. "The drink *must* be making you brave!"

Above their heads the clock of St Chad had tolled six.

"I must be off to the West End," Mr Iachimo said. "And you had better run home to supper. Till tomorrow, then – and a thousand, thousand thanks for your help."

He gave her a deep, foreign bow and limped, much faster than usual, away down the hill.

"Oh, do let it work," Emmeline thought, looking after him.

Then she ran home to Mrs Vaughan's.

Supper was over; Colin, thank goodness, did not come in, and Mrs Vaughan wanted to get through and be off; Emmeline bolted down her food, washed the plates, and was dismissed to the streets again.

As she ran up to the churchyard wall, with her fingers tight clenched round the precious little flask, a worrying thought suddenly struck her.

The magic drink had mead in it. Suppose the mead were to give Mr Iachimo hiccups? But there must be very little mead in such a tiny drop, she consoled herself; the risk could not be great.

When she pulled her book from the hole in the wall a sound met her ears that made her smile with relief: old Scrawny's mew of greeting, rather creaking and scratchy, as he dragged himself yawning, one leg at a time, from a clump of ivy on top of the wall.

"*There* you are, Scrawny! If you knew how I'd been worrying about you!"

She tucked him under one arm, put the book under the other, and made her way to the telephone box. Scrawny settled on her feet for another nap, and she opened *The Ancient History of Kimball's Green*. Only one chapter remained to be read; she turned to it and became absorbed. St Chad's clock ticked solemnly round overhead.

When Emmeline finally closed the book, tears were running down her face.

"Oh, Scrawny – they didn't win! They *lost*! King Cunobel's men were all killed – and the Druids too, defending the stronghold. Every one of them. Oh, how can I bear it? Why did it have to happen, Scrawny?"

Scrawny made no answer, but he laid his chin over her ankle. At that moment the telephone bell rang.

Emmeline stared at the instrument in utter consternation. Scrawny sprang up; the fur along his back *slowly* raised, and his ears flattened. The bell went on ringing.

"But," whispered Emmeline, staring at the

broken black receiver, "it's out of order. It *can't* ring! It's never rung! What shall I do, Scrawny?"

By now, Scrawny had recovered. He sat himself down again and began to wash. Emmeline looked up and down the empty street. Nobody came. The bell went on ringing.

At the same time, down below the hill and some distance off, in Wansea High Street, ambulance attendants were carefully lifting an old man off the pavement and laying him on a stretcher.

"Young brutes," said a bystander to a policeman who was taking notes. "It was one of those gangs of young hooligans from up Kimball's Green way; I'd know several of them again if I saw them. They set on him – it's the old street musician who comes up from there too. Seems he was coming home early tonight, and the boys jumped on him – you wouldn't think they'd bother with a poor fellow like him, he can't have much worth stealing."

But the ambulance men were gathering up handfuls of half-crowns and two-shilling pieces which had rolled from Mr Iachimo's pockets; there were notes as well, a pound, even five- and ten-pound notes. And a broken flute.

"It was certainly worth their while tonight," the policeman said. "He must have done a lot better than usual."

"He was a game old boy – fought back like a lion; marked some of them, I shouldn't wonder. They had to leave him and run for it. Will he be all right?"

"We'll see," said the ambulance man, closing the doors.

"I'd better answer it," Emmeline said at last. She picked up the receiver, trembling as if it might give her a shock.

"Hello?" she whispered.

And a voice – a faint, hoarse, distant voice – said,

"This is King Cunobel. I cannot speak for long. I am calling to warn you. There is danger on the way – great danger coming towards you and your friend. Take care! Watch well!"

Emmeline's lips parted. She could not speak.

"There is danger — danger!" the voice repeated. Then the line went silent.

Emmeline stared from the silent telephone to the cat at her feet.

"Did you hear it too, Scrawny?"

Scrawny gazed at her impassively, and washed behind his ear.

Then Emmeline heard the sound of running feet. The warning had been real. She pushed the book into her pocket and was about to pick up Scrawny, but hesitated, with her fingers on the little flask.

"Maybe I ought to drink it, Scrawny? Better that than have it fall into the enemy's hands. Should I? Yes, I will! Here, you must have a drop too."

She laid a wet finger on Scrawny's nose; out came his pink tongue at once. Then she drained the bottle, picked up Scrawny, opened the door, and ran.

Turning back once more to look she could

see a group of dark figures coming after her down the street. She heard someone shout,

"That's her, and she's got the cat too! Come on!"

But beyond, behind and *through* her pursuers, Emmeline caught a glimpse of something else: a high, snow-covered hill, higher than the hill she knew, crowned with great bare trees. And on either side of her, among and in front of the dark houses, as if she were seeing two pictures, one printed on top of the other, were still more trees, and little thatched stone houses. Thin animals with red eyes slunk silently among the huts. Just a glimpse she had, of the two worlds, one behind the other, and then she had reached Mrs Vaughan's doorstep and turned to face the attackers.

Colin Vaughan was in the lead; his face, bruised, cut, and furious, showed its ugly intention as plainly as a raised club.

"Give me that damn cat. I've had enough from you and your friends. I'm going to wring its neck."

But Emmeline stood at bay; her eyes blazed

defiance and so did Scrawny's; he bared his fangs at Colin like a sabre-tooth tiger.

Emmeline said clearly, "Don't you dare lay a finger on me, Colin Vaughan. Just don't you dare touch me!"

He actually flinched, and stepped back half a pace; his gang shuffled back behind him.

At this moment Mrs Vaughan came up the hill; not at her usual smart pace but slowly, plodding, as if she had no heart in her.

"Clear out, the lot of you," she said angrily. "Poor old Mr Iachimo's in the Wansea Hospital, thanks to you. Beating up old men! That's all you're good for. Go along, scram, before I set the back of my hand to some of you. Beat it!"

"But we were going to wring the cat's neck. You wanted me to do that," Colin protested.

"Oh, what do I care about the blame cat?" she snapped, turning to climb the steps, and came face to face with Emmeline.

"Well, don't *you* stand there like a lump," Mrs Vaughan said angrily. "Put the blasted animal down and get to bed!"

"I'm not going to bed," Emmeline said. "I'm

not going to live with you any more."

"Oh, indeed? And where are you going then?" said Mrs Vaughan, completely astonished.

"I'm going to see poor Mr Yakkymo. And then I'm going to find someone who'll take me and Scrawny, some place where I shall be happy. I'm never coming back to your miserable house again."

"Oh, well, suit yourself," Mrs Vaughan grunted. "You're not the only one. I've just heard: fifty years in this place and then fourteen days' notice to quit; in two weeks the bulldozers are coming."

She went indoors.

But Emmeline had not listened; clutching Scrawny, brushing past the gang as if they did not exist, she ran for the last time down the dark streets of Kimball's Green.

When Hitler Stole Pink Rabbit

Judith Kerr

There is soon to be a general election in Germany. Adolf Hitler's Nazi party is expected to win. It is a dangerous time to be Jewish, like Anna and Max's family. Their father, a famous writer critical of Hitler, has already had to flee the country. Now Anna, Max and their mother are escaping by train to join him in Switzerland. They have taken only what is vital to the journey, their mother clutching a bag with a camel on it which has their passports hidden inside.

Before they reach Switzerland, they must stop for the night in Stuttgart . . .

Anna sleepily put on her coat, and soon she and Max were sitting on the luggage at the entrance of Stuttgart station while Mama went to get a taxi. The rain was still pelting down, drumming on the station roof and falling like a shiny curtain between them and the dark square in front of them. It was cold. At last Mama came back.

"What a place!" she cried. "They've got some sort of a strike on – something to do with the elections – and there are no taxis. But you see that blue sign over there?" On the opposite side of the square there was a bluish gleam among the wet. "That's a hotel," said Mama. "We'll just take what we need for the night and make a dash for it."

With the bulk of the luggage safely deposited they struggled across the ill-lit square. The case Anna was carrying kept banging across her leg and the rain was so heavy that she could hardly see. Once she missed her footing and stepped into a deep puddle so that her feet were soaked. But at last they were in the dry. Mama booked rooms

for them and then she and Max had
something to eat. Anna was tired. She went
straight to bed and to sleep.

In the morning they got up while it was still
dark. "We'll soon see Papa," said Anna as
they ate breakfast in the dimly-lit dining-
room. Nobody else was up yet and the sleepy-
eyed waiter seemed to grudge them the stale
rolls and coffee which he banged down in
front of them. Mama waited until he had
gone back into the kitchen. Then she said,
"Before we get to Zurich and see Papa we
have to cross the frontier between Germany
and Switzerland."

"Do we have to get off the train?" asked
Max.

"No," said Mama. "We just stay in our
compartment and then a man will come and
look at our passports – just like the ticket
inspector. But" – and she looked at both
children in turn – "this is very important.
When the man comes to look at our passports
I want neither of you to say anything. Do you
understand? Not a word."

"Why not?" asked Anna.

"Because otherwise the man will say 'What a horrible talkative little girl, I think I'll take away her passport'," said Max who was always bad-tempered when he had not had enough sleep.

"Mama!" appealed Anna. "He wouldn't really – take away our passports, I mean?"

"No . . . no, I don't suppose so," said Mama. "But just in case – Papa's name is so well known – we don't want to draw attention to ourselves in any way. So when the man comes – not a word. Remember – not a single, solitary word!"

Anna promised to remember.

The rain had stopped at last and it was quite easy walking back across the square to the station. The sky was just beginning to brighten and now Anna could see that there were election posters everywhere. Two or three people were standing outside a place marked Polling Station, waiting for it to open. She wondered if they were going to vote, and for whom.

The train was almost empty and they had

a whole compartment to themselves until a lady with a basket got in at the next station. Anna could hear a sort of shuffling inside the basket – there must be something alive in it. She tried to catch Max's eye to see if he had heard it too, but he was still feeling cross and was frowning out of the window. Anna began to feel bad-tempered too and to remember that her head ached and that her boots were still wet from last night's rain.

"When do we get to the frontier?" she asked.

"I don't know," said Mama. "Not for a while yet." Anna noticed that her fingers were squashing the camel's face again.

"In about an hour, d'you think?" asked Anna.

"You never stop asking questions," said Max, although it was none of his business. "Why can't you shut up?"

"Why can't you?" said Anna. She was bitterly hurt and cast around for something wounding to say. At last she came out with, "I wish I had a sister!"

"I wish I didn't!" said Max.

"Mama!" wailed Anna.

"Oh, for goodness sake, stop it!" cried Mama. "Haven't we got enough to worry about?" She was clutching the camel bag and peering into it every so often to see if the passports were still there.

Anna wriggled crossly in her seat. Everybody was horrible. The lady with the basket had produced a large chunk of bread with some ham and was eating it. No one said anything for a long time. Then the train began to slow down.

"Excuse me," said Mama, "but are we coming to the Swiss frontier?"

The lady with the basket munched and shook her head.

"There, you see!" said Anna to Max. "Mama is asking questions too!"

Max did not even bother to answer but rolled his eyes up to heaven. Anna wanted to kick him, but Mama would have noticed.

The train stopped and started again, stopped and started again. Each time Mama asked if it was the frontier, and each time the lady with the basket shook her head. At last when the train slowed down yet again at the sight of a cluster of buildings, the lady with the basket said, "I dare say we're coming to it now."

They waited in silence while the train stood in the station. Anna could hear voices and the doors of other compartments opening and shutting. Then footsteps in the corridor. Then the door of their own compartment slid open and the passport inspector came in. He had a uniform rather like a ticket inspector and a large brown moustache.

He looked at the passport of the lady with the basket, nodded, stamped it with a little rubber stamp, and gave it back to her. Then he turned to Mama. Mama handed him the passports and smiled. But the hand with which she was holding her handbag was squeezing the camel into terrible contortions. The man examined the passports. Then he looked at Mama to see if it was the same face as on the passport photograph, then at Max and then at Anna. Then he got out his rubber stamp. Then he remembered something and looked at the passports again. Then at last he stamped them and gave them back to Mama.

"Pleasant journey," he said as he opened the door of the compartment.

Nothing had happened. Max had frightened her all for nothing.

"There, you see . . .!" cried Anna, but Mama gave her such a look that she stopped.

The passport inspector closed the door behind him.

"We're still in Germany," said Mama.

Anna could feel herself blushing scarlet.

Mama put the passports back in the bag. There was silence. Anna could hear whatever it was scuffling in the basket, the lady munching another piece of bread and ham, doors opening and shutting further along the train. It seemed to last for ever.

Then the train started, rolling a few hundred yards and stopped again. More opening and shutting of doors, this time more quickly. Voices saying, "Customs . . . anything to declare . . . ?" A different man came into the compartment. Mama and the lady both said they had nothing to declare and he made a mark with chalk on all their luggage, even on the lady's basket. Another wait, then a whistle and at last they started again. This time the train gathered speed and went on chugging steadily through the countryside.

After a long time Anna asked, "Are we in Switzerland yet?"

"I think so. I'm not sure," said Mama.

The lady with the basket stopped chewing. "Oh yes," she said comfortably, "this is Switzerland. We're in Switzerland now – this is my country."

It was marvellous.

"Switzerland!" said Anna. "We're really in Switzerland!"

"About time too!" said Max and grinned.

Mama put the camel bag down on the seat beside her and smiled and smiled.

"Well!" she said. "Well! We'll soon be with Papa."

Anna suddenly felt quite silly and light-headed. She wanted to do or say something extraordinary and exciting but could think of nothing at all – so she turned to the Swiss lady and said, "Excuse me, but what have you got in that basket?"

"That's my mogger," said the lady in her soft country voice.

For some reason this was terribly funny. Anna, biting back her laughter, glanced at Max and found that he too was almost in convulsions.

"What's a . . . what's a mogger?" she asked as the lady folded back the lid of the basket, and before anyone could answer there was a screech of "Meeee", and the head of a scruffy black tomcat appeared out of the opening.

At this Anna and Max could contain themselves no longer. They fell about with laughter.

"He answered you!" gasped Max. "You said, 'What's a mogger' and he said—"

"Meee!" screamed Anna.

"Children, children!" said Mama, but it was no good – they could not stop laughing. They laughed at everything they saw, all the way to Zurich. Mama apologized to the lady but she said she did not mind – she knew high spirits when she saw them. Any time they looked like flagging Max only had to say,

"What's a mogger?" and Anna cried, "Meee!" and they were off all over again. They were still laughing on the platform in Zurich when they were looking for Papa.

Anna saw him first. He was standing by a bookstall. His face was white and his eyes were searching the crowds milling round the train.

"Papa!" she shouted. "Papa!"

He turned and saw them. And then Papa, who was always so dignified, who never did anything in a hurry, suddenly ran towards them. He put his arms round Mama and hugged her. Then he hugged Anna and Max. He hugged and hugged them all and would not let them go.

"I couldn't see you," said Papa. "I was afraid . . ."

"I know," said Mama.

Night School

Robert Swindells

Things had started to go missing from school recently, just little things like pencils and rulers, so far. They seemed to vanish overnight, which was odd, so when Lucy's mother found that Lucy had left her leotard at school that Friday, she wasn't very pleased.

"You must go straight back and fetch it," she said, even though it was nearly seven o'clock by then. "It's not far, so don't be long."

Lucy's friend Jen was with her, so they went together. By the time they reached the school gates the porch light was on, and light showed through one small window too, but most of the place was in darkness.

Jen nodded towards the lighted window.

"That'll be Mrs Berry, the caretaker, but the cleaners will have gone. Come on."

They hurried into school and were just about to cross the dark hall when Lucy seized Jen's sleeve and pointed.

"Look!"

On the far side of the hall a classroom door was opening and two shadowy figures appeared. They looked like children, except that their heads seemed too big and glowed faintly green. As the friends watched, the two figures went back into the classroom, closing the door behind them.

"They're just kids," Jen breathed.

"Are you sure?" whispered Lucy. "Those oversize heads, sort of glowing?"

"Sure," Jen replied. "They're not ghosts or monsters, if that's what you mean. They're people. *I'm* not scared of them – are you?"

"A bit," admitted Lucy. "But my leotard's in that room. Will you go first, Jen?"

Jen took a deep breath and strode across the hall with Lucy at her heels. She would fling open the door, and then they would see what they would see. After all, these creatures had no business here, creeping about in the dark. Whoever they were, they'd be as scared of Lucy and herself as the girls were of them – more scared, probably.

The door had a small glass panel, and through it the girls could see figures moving about in the gloom. Then they must have heard a noise, because all the figures froze. There was a clatter and scrape of chairs as Jen bravely flung back the door and switched on the lights.

They both blinked at the sudden brightness. But when they opened their eyes again – the figures had gone! Books, pencils and sheets of paper lay on some of the tables, the chairs stood higgledy-piggledy and two had fallen over, but there was nobody there at all. At least Lucy's leotard was still there, folded up neatly on her table. She picked it up.

"But they were here!" Jen cried. "You saw them, didn't you?"

Lucy gulped and nodded. "Yes. There were at least six. They must have been ghosts, Jen – only ghosts could vanish like that."

Jen shook her head. "Ghosts don't read

books or knock chairs over. They were real, like you and me, only . . . Can you hear something?" Lucy listened. Somewhere, water was running. "Somebody's in the washrooms. Come on!"

She switched off the lights again, then they tiptoed out of the classroom and towards the washrooms.

Lucy stopped. "It's coming from the boys' side," she whispered. "We can't go in there."

"Of course we can. You don't think there'll be boys there at this time of night, do you?"

They crept through the open doorway and peered round the corner. A shadowy form bent over the end washbasin, washing its hands. Close to where they stood a chair was against the wall. On the chair was a large, roundish object which glowed faintly green.

"Oh Jen – look," moaned Lucy. "It's taken its head off."

"No it hasn't. It's some sort of helmet. I bet they all wear them – that's what makes their heads look so big."

"So what should we do?"

"This." Before Lucy could protest, Jen had switched on the lights.

It was a boy. At least, it looked like a boy. He was dark-haired and slender, and about the same height as Lucy. His eyes were dark and his skin a yellowish brown. He wore black jeans and silver trainers and a black, quilted jacket with the sleeves rolled up. As the washroom flooded with light he stared at the two girls, then past them to where the helmet rested on the chair.

"Who are you?" asked Jen.

"Kit." The boy's eyes were on the helmet.

"Where are you from?"

"Not where. When. Gimme headgear."

Jen shook her head. "Not till you tell us where you come from and what you're doing in our school."

"My school too. Your school, 1995. My school, 2495. Five hundred years from now, yes?"

Jen's eyes narrowed. "Are you saying you're from the future?"

"Print that."

"Pardon?"

"Sorry. I mean yes, that's right."

"We don't believe you, do we, Lucy?"

Lucy nodded rather nervously.

"I can't make you believe me. OK if I dry?"

"Sure." Jen nodded towards the helmet. "You can have this in a minute."

He walked away from them and dried his hands under the hand-dryer.

When the dryer stopped and he tugged down his sleeves – "Where did the others go?" asked Lucy quietly.

"Back."

"Where? I mean, one second they were

there, the next they'd vanished. How did they do that?"

"Escape key," said Kit. He pointed to the helmet. "In there."

"Oh. Is that why you didn't vanish too?"

"Print that. 'Headgear will be worn at all times.' A rule. I broke the rule. Nokay?"

"Nokay?"

"Nokay. That means stupid. Thick, yes?"

Both girls nodded, smiling.

"You," said Kit. "Why you here at night?"

"We came to collect my leotard," said Lucy. "Before it got moved, or disappeared," she added pointedly.

"Moved is not OK," said Kit, frowning. "Disappear is not OK. The rule says, 'Nothing to be taken away from its time or place.' But some kids break the rules. It's rom."

"What's rom?"

Kit smiled for the first time. "Rom means something they can't help. It's just the way they are."

"But if you live in Fenton like us, and this is your school, why do you use such funny words? Why don't you talk the same as us?"

99

Kit smiled again. "Because some words go out of use and new ones are invented, of course. We're finding out about ancient Fenton. For school. We wanted to see what school was like in 1995."

"Wow!" cried Jen. "Do you mean you have a time-machine or something?"

"Oh yes," said Kit. "Every school has. Kids can travel to any century they like and see how people lived. Adults can as well. We always do it at night so the people don't see, but sometimes we make a mistake, like tonight, and somebody *does* see us. Kids come here all the time. A few steal things – pencils and rulers mostly. Small things we don't have in 2495." He grinned. "I'll tell you a secret, if you promise not to tell anyone else."

"We promise," said Lucy. "Don't we, Jen?" Jen nodded.

"OK. You know the stories you hear about ghosts and haunted places? Well – there's no such thing as ghosts. What people see is somebody like me, from the future. That's why ghosts are always seen at night, and why they vanish into thin air. OK?"

That was a relief, thought Lucy. She'd always been scared stiff of ghosts before, but she wouldn't be any more.

"Now gimme headgear," said Kit.

Jen pulled a face. "Not yet. There's millions of things I want to know first."

Kit smiled sadly. "It's dangerous," he said. "For me. If adults came, I would be captured. They would question me to find out about the future, and perform experiments on me too. They would never let me return to my own time."

"Oh, they would!" cried Lucy. "They couldn't be so cruel."

Kit smiled again. "You are wrong," he said. "Think of the cruel things people do to animals."

"No adults are going to come," Jen said. "Not until morning. Won't you stay just half an hour and talk?"

Kit shook his head. "I'd like to," he said. "I'd like to still be here in the morning so I could see the birds. We don't have birds."

"You don't have birds?" gasped Lucy. "Why not?"

Kit looked sheepish. "Well, really I shouldn't have told you that. It's against the rules. What happened was, people put stuff on the land to kill insects – chemical stuff – and it killed all the birds as well. And then the chemicals got washed to the sea and most of the fish died too."

"When did they do that?" asked Jen.

"They're doing it now," Kit replied. "They've been doing it for a long time, and they'll go on doing it."

"What if we tell everybody about the birds and fish?"

Kit laughed. "They won't listen. People do tell them, but they don't listen. They never will. Gimme headgear now." He held out his hands. "Please."

There was a crash outside, then a voice saying, "There's a light on over there." Then another voice, much louder, called out, "Lucy – are you in there, Lucy?"

Lucy gasped. "It's my dad," she hissed. "Quick, Jen – the helmet."

At the sound of the crash, Kit had darted towards the chair. He had almost reached it when Jen made a grab for it, intending to hand the helmet to him. As they collided the chair fell over and the helmet rolled across the floor. Lucy's father strode through the doorway, almost fell over it, and kicked it aside.

"Why has it taken so long?" he panted. "We've been worried sick."

Now Jen's father appeared in the doorway as well, followed by Mrs Berry. Jen and Kit scrambled to their feet. The boy backed off, staring at where the helmet lay in a corner by the door. Mrs Berry looked at him and frowned.

"I don't know who *he* is," she said. "He's not from this school."

"He's Kit. He's – not from around here," said Jen.

"We were talking," said Lucy. "We forgot the time."

"But who is he?" said Mrs Berry grimly. "That's what I'd like to know."

Jen's father looked at her. "Check around to see if anything's missing," he said. "If there is, we'll call the police."

103

"No, Dad!" Jen ran to her father and clung to his arm. "Don't call the police. Awful things will happen to him if you do. He's not a thief – honestly."

"Then what's he doing here at this time of night?" Lucy's father demanded. "And for that matter, why are you and Jennifer still here, Lucy? It shouldn't have taken all this time just to collect a leotard."

"Oh no you don't," Jen's father said as Kit suddenly made a dash towards the door, and tried to stop him.

Jen scooped up the helmet as Kit swerved to avoid her father's outstretched arm. "Here!" She tossed it to him and he was gone – through the doorway and out across the hall, with Lucy's father, Jen's father and Mrs Berry charging after him.

He swerved towards the classroom and cried out as Lucy's father loomed in front of him. He swerved again and ran, with the helmet tucked under his arm. As the three adults closed in on him, Kit made one last desperate swerve, burst open the classroom door and plunged into the gloom inside.

Lucy's father reached the classroom first and promptly switched on the lights. Then he glanced around. His mouth fell open. He shook his head and rubbed his eyes. Mrs Berry and Jen's father gazed over his shoulders into the empty room.

"But he can't just have vanished!" exclaimed Jen's father.

Lucy and Jen had caught up with them now.

"Oh, but he could," said Lucy. "You see – really he's a sort of ghost, isn't he, Jen?"

"Oh, yes," agreed Jen happily. "They all are."

Aliens Don't Eat Bacon Sandwiches

Helen Dunmore

My brother Dan has been making his own bacon sandwiches since he was ten years old. It's not that he likes cooking that much – it's just that no one else knows how to make the perfect bacon sandwich. He'd get everything ready by the cooker first. Bacon, bread, tomatoes, ketchup, sharp knife. The bacon had to be fried fast, so it was crisp but not dried up. He'd lay it on one slice of soft white bread, smear it with ketchup, cover it with tomato slices, and then clap a matching white slice on top. Then he'd bite into it while the bacon was hot and the fat was soaking into the bread. Dad used to say that Dan would go to Mars and back if he thought there'd be a bacon sandwich at the end of it. Don't forget this. The bacon sandwich is important.

Then there was the portable telephone. We should never have bought it, Mum said. I mean, I like talking to my friends on the phone, but Dan was something else. He was never off it. When he came in from school he'd pick up the phone right away and call someone he'd only been talking to half an hour before. And they'd talk and talk and talk. Sometimes Mum would come in and stand there tapping her watch or mouthing "phone bill!" at him, but it never seemed to make much difference. Dan was a phone addict. I was cleaning my bike in the garden one day, and Mum and her friend Susie were talking about telephones and big bills and teenage kids. Susie said, "It's all right as long as you realize that teenagers aren't people at all really. They're aliens from outer space. That's why they spend all their time on the phone. They have to keep in contact with other aliens who come from the same planet."

I didn't take much notice of what Susie said at the time, but it came back to me later. Mum leaned back in her deckchair and laughed. She'd been out on a location all day, taking photographs: Mum's a photographer. She was working on a feature about corn circles. I expect you've seen pictures of them. Perfect circles in wheat, much too perfect to have been made by wind or rain. There were more of them than ever that year, and nobody knew how they came. At first the newspapers said it was a hoax. Reporters and photographers used to sit up and keep watch all night by cornfields, to catch the hoaxers. But they never did. Somehow they'd get sleepy and doze off and then when they jerked awake the circle would be there, just as round as if it had been drawn with a compass. Mum could have stayed the night too. She was working with a journalist friend who'd brought a tent along. Mum talked to Dan and me about it, then she decided not to stay. It was just a feeling she had that it wasn't a good idea. Dan and I always listened to Mum when she got feelings about things. Even I could remember how she'd said to Dad, just before he went on that last trip, "Do be careful, love. I've got a feeling about . . . I wish you weren't going."

Dad had worked for INTERSTEL airways, on the crash investigation team. He was an instrument specialist. This time he hadn't been investigating a crash, but several pilots had reported interference with their instruments over the Mojave Desert. They'd managed to correct the problems manually so far, but the airline was quietly panicking. Dad had been working on a computer model, trying to find some pattern in what was going on. I don't remember much about that time, but Dan told me later that Dad had been up most of the night the week before he left. He was really worried. All he said to Dan and Mum was that a pattern kept coming up, and he didn't like the look of it.

Mum's feeling was right. Dad's plane crashed not far from Coyote Lake. Something went wrong with the instruments, they said: there'd been massive distortions caused by what looked like a powerful electrical storm.

At least, that's what it looked like on the computer trace. But no storm showed up for hundreds of miles on the weather charts.

I asked Mum if she thought the corn circles really were made by aliens, like people said. She frowned, then she said, "I don't know, Tony. I don't believe that the circles are made by UFOs landing. That would be much too obvious. The feeling I have is that we're being teased. Or tricked. As if someone – or something – is trying to distract us from what they're really doing."

"What do you mean?"

"It's hard to explain, but try to put yourself in their place. If there really are aliens trying to get a foothold on our planet, I think they'd do it in a way we'd hardly even notice. There'd be changes, but not huge ones. After all there are millions of us on this planet, and only a few of them. They'd come in very gradually over the years. They wouldn't want to risk being noticed – not too soon."

"We'd be bound to notice, though, wouldn't we?"

"Not necessarily. Think of burglars. Some

break in through the front door with crow-bars, but others come in pairs pretending to be insurance salesmen. It's not till long after they've gone that you realize one of them's nipped upstairs and taken all your valuables. If there *were* aliens they wouldn't want to seem different. They'd want to seem like us. Part of normal life."

So Mum thought the corn circles were there to keep us busy. To stop us noticing what else was going on. I shivered.

Dan was fifteen and a half, and I was almost eleven. You wouldn't think we'd be friends as well as brothers, but we always had been. Dan told me things he'd never tell Mum. He knew I'd never grass on him. And if something made him sad he could tell me that too. He had a music centre for his fifteenth birthday, much better than the one downstairs in the sitting room. He'd lie on his bed and I'd lie on the floor and we'd listen to his music and he'd tell me about what was going on with his friends; not all of it, but some. Enough. Dan had a Saturday job, so he always had money. And he'd talk to me about Genevieve. He knew I liked her. He'd had girlfriends before, but Genevieve was different.

That was another clue I didn't pick up straight away. It was about five o'clock and Dan and I were home from school, but Mum wasn't back yet. The phone rang and I answered it. It was Genevieve. She asked how I was, the way she always did. She even remembered that I'd had to take my budgie to the vet, and asked if he was OK now. Then she said, "Is Dan there, Tony?"

"Yes, I'll just get him."

I turned round. Dan was lounging in the doorway, watching me.

"It's Genevieve," I said, holding the phone, but Dan didn't take it. He just kept on looking at me. It's hard to describe what happened next. I hadn't really been thinking about what was going on, because I was just doing something I'd done loads of times before, taking a call for Dan and passing it on to him. And since it was Genevieve I knew he'd be pleased. But he wasn't pleased this time. He didn't react at all. I felt as if I was searching Dan's face for someone who wasn't there, like you'd search an empty house for a light in the windows.

"It's *Genevieve!*" I hissed, thinking perhaps he hadn't heard, and wishing I'd pressed the silence button in case Genevieve had. But Dan just shook his head, very slightly, as if he was making fun of me. Or Genevieve. And I was left holding the phone.

"I'm sorry, Genevieve," I gabbled. "He just went out, I think. I mean, I thought he was here, but he isn't." It must have sounded like a lie, but Genevieve isn't a suspicious sort of person.

"Oh, that's OK, Tony," she said. "I'll try again later. See you," and she put the phone down. Her voice was just the same as always. You know how some people's voices make you feel that good things are about to happen? Genevieve had that sort of voice.

Dan's voice was cold and irritated. I couldn't believe I was hearing him right. "I wish she'd stop bothering me," he said.

"What?"

"You heard. I said I wish she'd stop bothering me. That girl really bugs me. If she calls again, say you don't know when I'll be back. No. Never mind. I'll take the phone."

He held his hand out for it. Darkness looked out of his eyes, and blankness. There was no Dan there at all. He took the phone and held it up as if he was going to dial straight away. The silver antenna poked out at the side of his head. I felt a shiver go through me. The antenna. Dan's dead eyes. Something scratched at the back of my mind, wanting to be let in:

"That's why they spend all their time on the phone, so they can keep in touch with all the other aliens..."

I stared at Dan and he stared back at me. Mocking, as if he knew something I didn't. And in a way... almost frightening. And then I heard Mum's key go into the front door lock.

Dan stopped looking at me. By the time Mum called hello to us, he was already on his way up the stairs, calling back "Homework" as he went. That was strange too. Dan usually made Mum a cup of coffee when she got in from work. His bedroom door banged with the sort of bang that tells everyone else to keep out. I waited to hear the music; Dan always turned on his music as soon as he got into his room. But nothing happened. It was absolutely silent, as if there was no Dan in there at all.

That was the first evening Dan didn't eat supper. He'd been into Burger King with Alex on his way back from school. Mum didn't bother about it: she was tired and upset because she and her journalist friend had had an argument with their editor. The editor didn't like the idea of aliens coming in secretly while we were all busy with the corn circles. He wasn't going to run the feature unless they changed it.

The next day Dan said he had to finish a piece of coursework and could he take a sandwich and a glass of milk up to his room. I don't remember all the excuses for not eating after that, at breakfast and tea and supper. They were never the same twice. Dan had always been clever, but now he was cunning too. He emptied his wastepaper basket every day now, so there was no chance of Mum finding the sandwiches he hadn't eaten. It was hard to know how much Mum had noticed. She never said anything, and she carried on giving Dan dinner money as usual.

It was three nights after the phone call from Genevieve that I couldn't sleep. My bedroom was next to Dan's, but I hadn't been into Dan's room for three days. Have you ever seen two magnets fighting one another with an invisible forcefield between them? There was one of those forcefields at Dan's bedroom door. You couldn't see it, you couldn't touch it, but it was there. Even Mum found excuses not to go in there. She was collecting the dirty washing one afternoon when Dan was late home, and she said, "I ought to have a sock-search under Dan's bed," but she didn't go in. She hesitated by his door, then she said, "No. He's old enough to sort out his own dirty washing," and she walked past into my room to change my duvet cover.

I kept turning over and over in bed. I was used to falling asleep to the sound of Dan's music, and I couldn't settle down in the silence. What was he doing? Was he sitting there? Reading? Working? I knew there wasn't anyone else in the room, though usually Dan had his friends round a lot, and often they stayed late. None of his friends had been round for the past three days. And I don't know what he'd said to Genevieve, but she hadn't called again. I tossed back the duvet and it flumped on to the floor. I found myself tiptoeing across the carpet, easing the door-handle down, pulling the door open very gently. The landing light was on. Everything was quiet and Mum's door was shut too. 12:37 on my watch. She'd be asleep. My heart thudded as I crept close to Dan's door. Yes, it was still there, the invisible hand pushing me away, saying I wasn't wanted there. But I wasn't going to take any notice this time. This was Dan, my brother. I took a breath, and touched his door-handle. Something fizzed on my fingers, like a tiny electric charge, like a rush of static electricity. I pulled my hand away and stepped back. Then I stopped myself.

"It's only Dan," I told myself fiercely. "It's only Dan."

This time the prickle of electricity wasn't so bad, or perhaps it was because I was expecting it. Very gently I pushed the handle down. It didn't squeak or click. Then I pushed the door. As it opened a narrow strip of light fell from the landing into the darkness of Dan's room. It lit up Dan's bed, which was opposite the door. It lit up Dan, who was sitting up on the bed, fully dressed, reading. Reading in the dark. It lit up Dan's eyes as he turned to me, not at all surprised, as if he'd been expecting me. As if he'd seen me through the door.

"Hi," he said, and turned a page.

There was only one switch for the main light, and it was by the door. It was off. I opened the door wider, so that more light came in, and walked across to Dan's bed. Casually, I touched his bedside light. It was cold. It hadn't been on at all. He'd really been reading in the dark – unless he'd been pretending? Unless he was trying to trick me and he'd been sitting there with the book, waiting for me to come in? But then how had he known I was going to come in?

There wasn't an answer. There was only Dan sitting on his bed. He didn't look as if he liked me much.

"I can't sleep," I said. "I'm going down to make some hot chocolate. Do you want some?"

"No," said Dan. A week ago he'd have come down with me so I wouldn't make too much noise and wake up Mum. He'd have whipped up the chocolate, the way he does. Suddenly I had an idea.

"I'm going to make a bacon sandwich," I said, and waited for Dan to say what he always said: "You make a bacon sandwich?

Don't make me laugh. Let the man from the army do it." And then he'd make it for me.

He didn't. But something went over his face. Just for a second, there was a flicker of the real Dan, and as soon as I saw it I knew for sure that whoever else had been there the past three days, it hadn't been Dan. Then his face went back to the not-Dan face. The alien face. I felt the back of my neck prickle. Maybe it was the electricity, tingling around the room. Out of the corner of my eye I caught a movement. It was the minute hand of Dan's electric wall-clock, racing crazily round and round in a perfect circle. The thing inside my brother looked straight at me, daring me to say what I'd seen. The prickle ran up my arms and down. I'd run into a storm, just the way Dad had done, only here it wasn't as strong. There was only one of them here. I shook my head to clear the buzzing of my thoughts. Dan needed me.

"I really fancy a bacon sandwich," I said again. "We've got all the stuff. White bread, tomatoes, ketchup – and Mum bought some back bacon yesterday."

Something struggled in his eyes again, like the ghost of my brother. It wasn't winning. Dan wanted so much to come back, but he couldn't. There was something else there, something alien, and it was too strong for Dan. It meant to stay, and it meant to keep Dan out of his own body. But at least now I felt I knew what I was fighting. What we were fighting. Dan hadn't eaten anything for three days. I knew he hadn't. He must be hungry. Whatever was in him now didn't need food, not our earth food. But Dan did. And Dan would do anything for a bacon sandwich. Perhaps, if I could take him by surprise somehow, and get him to eat – could that break whatever power this thing had over him? I didn't know, but it was worth trying.

"See you downstairs if you change your mind," I said.

Our neighbours have a baby which cries in the night, so Mum goes to bed with cotton wool in her ears. Even so, I moved quietly as I lit the gas, got out the heavy frying pan, found bacon and tomatoes in the fridge, rummaged in the cupboard for ketchup. I just hoped the smell of frying bacon wouldn't wake her. I put the frying pan on, melted a bit of fat, and lowered the bacon on the slice. It fizzled. After a minute the first tantalizing wisp of the smell of frying bacon began to wreathe round the kitchen. Soon it would be through the door, then up the stairs, then under Dan's door. I turned up the heat carefully. I didn't want it to burn. The bacon spluttered, making a friendly sound in the kitchen. I laid the bread ready, and the sliced tomatoes, and the ketchup bottle. A drop of hot fat sparked on to the back of my hand and I sucked it away. Dan. Dan. Dan.

"Dan'd go to Mars and back if he thought he'd get a bacon sandwich at the end of it," Dad used to say. That was before Dad went.

The kitchen door opened. Dan walked slowly, as if he was pushing through something heavy. His face was pale, and it wasn't smooth and hard any more, the way it had been the past three days. It looked crumpled, as if he was trying to remember something.

"Your sandwich is nearly ready," I said. I

took the bacon off the heat, slid the slices out of the pan and laid them across the bread. I layered on the tomato and squeezed out just the right amount of ketchup. Then I cut the sandwich in half. Dan watched me all the time. I lifted my half, and took a bite. I saw him lick his lips, but he was shivering, as if he felt cold. And things were moving behind his eyes, as if they were fighting for space there.

"Dan," I said. "Your sandwich is getting cold."

His hands had dropped to his sides. They looked heavy. He didn't have the strength even to lift his hands, because all his strength was going into that fight inside him, between the Dan who was my brother and the stranger who wanted to make his home inside my brother's body. And that stranger was hanging on, tooth and claw. It wasn't going to let go easily. I knew now for sure that it was nothing human that was looking at me out of Dan's eyes. It had come from far away, and all it cared about was its resting-place. It was here for a purpose. It didn't care for Dan, or me or any of us. All it cared about was what it

needed. Dan would never eat or sleep again if it had its way.

"Dan," I said again. It felt as if his name was all I had. I came up close to him with his half of the sandwich still in my hand. He backed off a step or two, but then he didn't go any farther. I knew it was the real Dan who wanted to stay.

Suddenly I remembered something from far back, when I was sick with tonsilitis, not long after Dad died. It was when I was about six, I think. I had to take medicine four times a day, and I hated it. I used to press my lips tight shut and Mum couldn't make me swallow it. Then Dad took the spoon. He didn't seem worried, like Mum, and he didn't have any doubt that I'd open my mouth. He just put the spoon near my lips, without trying to push it into my mouth, and he said, "Come on, babes. Do it for me." And I did, every time, four times a day till I was better. The words had been like magic to me then, when I was a little kid. Would they work now? Could they be the one thing that would bring Dan back and help him to fight off that powerful and lonely thing which had come to make its home in him?

I held the bacon sandwich up to Dan's mouth. His face was sweaty and he was breathing hard, as if he'd been running a long way.

"Come on, babes," I whispered. "Do it for me."

I held my breath. I said it again, but silently. Then, like something in slow motion, Dan's mouth opened. I could see how hungry he was. How much he wanted to come home. I felt the electric prickle again, the one I'd felt when I first tried to open Dan's door. It was stronger now. It was trying to beat up a storm. It was fighting me, as well as Dan. But this time it wasn't going to win. Dan bit down. He bit into the white bread, the bacon which was still hot, the juicy tomato. I saw the marks of his teeth in the bread. He chewed, and he swallowed the bacon sandwich. Then I looked at him and it was like looking at a house where all the lights have come on at once after it's been empty for a long time. His hands weren't heavy any more. He grasped the sandwich, bit again, and in a minute he'd finished it.

"You going to make me another, Tony, or have I got to show you how the man from the army makes a bacon sandwich?" he asked, and he smiled.

I didn't even jump when Mum opened the kitchen door. I knew it was her, not the thing which had been here and which was gone now, away through lonely space and places I couldn't begin to imagine, looking for somewhere else to make its home. Mum pulled the cotton wool out of her ears.

"You boys," she said. "I should have known. I was dreaming about bacon sandwiches."

I don't know how Dan made it up with Genevieve, but the next day she was round at our house again. Dan's bedroom door was open, and his music was throbbing through the house. Mum didn't tell him to turn it down. She was in a wonderful mood because the editor had rung her back. He'd changed his mind and he was going to run the story about the corn circles in the way Mum and her friend wanted. For some reason he'd suddenly come to think it was worth printing the theory about aliens operating like bogus insurance salesmen, distracting us with corn circles and stealing our valuables when we weren't looking.

I asked Mum, "Does the editor have kids?"

"Yes, he's got a teenage daughter. She's been a bit of a problem lately, apparently – he was telling me."

Mum glanced round, saw Dan was laughing with Genevieve, and whispered, "His daughter's been acting a bit like Dan has these past few days, I think. But he says she's got over it too."

Genevieve stayed to supper, and you can guess what we ate. While we were eating it, I thought of what had happened the night before, in our midnight kitchen.

"Aliens don't eat bacon sandwiches," I thought, looking at my brother.

Crocodiles on the Mind

Rob Marsh

Benny was aware of the awful smell even before he began shivering violently with the cold. He groaned and tried hard to roll over and free his trapped arm, but one of his legs refused to co-operate and the soil above him pressed down against his shoulder, making all but the smallest moves impossible. With some effort he managed to slide a hand down his injured leg. Just below the knee the skin felt ragged and torn, although he could still move his foot. Fortunately, there was no pain. Deadened by the cold, he thought. For a few seconds he lay wrapped in the darkness, wondering. Then, slowly, the awful truth came back to him . . .

That morning, Benny, his friend Johno

129

Johnson and Johno's mum and dad had left Durban very early. They had taken the N2 coastal road north towards Stanger and Richards Bay into KwaZulu and had turned off the highway just past the Mkuze Game Reserve. At around eleven they were on their way to the forestland of the Ndumu Game Reserve, on the southern bank of the Usutu river on the Mozambique border.

By midday the sun was beating down and as they came closer to Ndumu the area became a patchwork of sandy plains, lakelets and small pans. Some of the stretches of water were crystal clear, but those which were fed by the muddy overflow from local rivers, looked more like dirty puddles. The land was flat and the area was teeming with wildlife.

By two o'clock Benny and Johno were inside the reserve. They had unpacked the car, erected the tent under the shade of a Fever tree and were ready to go exploring. But before Mr Johnson would let them go off on their own, he insisted on making sure they knew exactly what the ground rules were.

"You just watch what you're doing round

here," he warned. "The animals are wild and the river's full of crocodiles. And whatever you do, don't go out of the camp."

Johno took a step back and held his hands up in surrender. He was innocent - until proven guilty. "Don't you worry, Dad, we'll take care."

Mr Johnson who knew from experience just how much faith he could put in his son's assurances, squinted at him from under a floppy white hat. His mouth remained set in a serious expression. He was not convinced . . .

Shifting his gaze he said, "Make sure he doesn't do anything stupid, Benny." Behind Mr Johnson, Mrs Johnson who had been carrying a red sleeping bag to the tent, had stopped to listen.

Benny stared back at them both and tried to look more confident than he felt. He couldn't understand why they were looking at him for support. Didn't they know their son at all by now? He was completely unpredictable!

"We'll be careful, Mr Johnson," Benny answered reluctantly. He hoped he sounded convincing.

Somehow he felt like a traitor.

Johno's dad seemed to relax a little, and at Benny's shoulder Johno's smile stretched from ear to ear. "Very careful, Dad," he echoed.

The two boys made their way to the boundary of the camp and began walking along the fence, occasionally stopping to peer through the mesh. It was only when they were out of sight of the buildings that Benny realized his friend was searching for something, rather than simply admiring the landscape.

"What are you looking for?" he asked finally.

Johno didn't raise his eyes from the ground. "The last time I was here, there was a hole in the fence. If we're lucky it'll still be there."

Benny opened his mouth to protest but Johno was already on his knees scratching away at the grass. A second later he was on his belly wriggling into a small hollow underneath the wire. He stood up in the waist-high grass on the far side of the fence.

"Come on through," he said, dusting

himself off, carefully.

Through the trees behind Johno, Benny could just make out the sparkle of water in the distance. His heart began to pound.

"Come back in, Johno. It's dangerous out there. Stop fooling around."

"Dangerous, why?"

"There're wild animals. Crocodiles. You heard your dad . . ."

But Johno wasn't convinced. "It's not dangerous, not if you're careful. I should know, I've been here before."

Benny's heart sank. All the trees and bushes on the other side of the fence, that a moment before had looked so ordinary, suddenly seemed dark and threatening.

"Please, Johno, you've had your fun now, come back over this side."

Benny did his best to smile. After all, he could take a joke with the best of them. But Johno wasn't joking. "I want to go down to the river," he said. Benny felt his mouth go dry. Of all the horrible things in nature, crocodiles were the worst. The way they just lay there, hidden in the water, beady eyes staring. Just waiting to pounce . . .

In a documentary Benny had once seen, a man in khaki shorts and bush shirt had held a baby crocodile up to the camera for everyone to see, and then talked about how fast they moved. There had even been film of a crocodile snatching a goat with lightning speed, and dragging it back to the river. He remembered the helpless animal bleating in terror just before it vanished beneath the surface. The water had frothed for a moment and then gone still.

"We've got to keep away from the water. It's dangerous," Benny explained.

"Not if we're careful."

John wasn't scared, wasn't concerned even, which made Benny marvel at his courage.

He made one last attempt at reason. "But you heard what your dad said . . ."

"I said I'd be careful. I am being careful. I'm just being careful on this side of the fence. I just want to go down to the water, that's all."

"And then you'll come back?"

"Of course."

Benny remembered the promise Johno's

father had drawn from him. Even though he had been forced to give his word, he still felt some responsibility to his friend.

"If I come through we'll just go there and back."

Johno flashed his teeth. "All right," he agreed.

"Just there and back, you promise?" Benny repeated then wriggled under the fence.

By the time the two boys set out for the river, Benny's heart was beating like a drum.

The undergrowth was matted and tangled and the crunch of their footsteps, as they crashed through the thicket of dry leaves and dead sticks, disturbed the silence. Benny stumbled over a small boulder and went sprawling on to the ground. Grunting, he heaved himself up and then paused to catch his breath before setting off again. Never before had his legs felt so heavy.

At the river's edge there was a small clearing and a tiny beach of white sand which fringed the reedy shoreline. About thirty metres away, on the far side of the slow-moving river was a strip of sand similar to their own. Beyond it, the forest continued as far as the eye could see. Further down the river, heat waves shimmered over the water. It was deathly quiet. Benny shivered.

"Right," Benny said, "we've seen the river, now let's go back again."

That was not Johno's intention. Shading his eyes with his hand he scanned the opposite shore for signs of animal life, but nothing moved. "I could do with a swim," he said finally. Benny watched in disbelief as he began pulling off his T-shirt. Benny knew that this spelt trouble.

"Come on, Johno," he pleaded, "don't joke. Let's go back to camp."

Johno was a great friend but when he got a bee in his bonnet or set his mind on something he could be as stubborn as a mule. Also, swimming in the river was strictly forbidden. He wasn't going to chance it.

Johno did not seem to have heard him. He removed his shoes and then, standing with hands on his hips and barefoot some distance from the water's edge, he surveyed the scene.

With a growing sense of panic Benny tried

reason once more. "Come on, Johno, your mum and dad will be waiting for us by now."

"You're not scared, are you, Benny?" he asked.

Of course he was scared, who wouldn't be? "Course not. But I'm not stupid either. There are crocodiles in that river."

Johno turned and stared at the water once again, this time carefully checking along the bank. "Are there? I can't see any."

"Just because you can't see them doesn't mean they're not there."

Johno smiled. "You've been reading too many horror stories, Benny. Crocodiles don't like places where the water is moving, didn't you know that? And, anyway, what do you think they're going to do, sit hidden in the water for an hour while we decide whether or not to take a swim? I'll bet there's not a crocodile for kilometres!"

Benny didn't want to get into an argument, not here anyway. "Johno, you've got to be mad if you go near that water," he said.

"I'll tell you what, Benny," Johno answered, "you swim across the river to the other bank and back with me and I'll never go under the fence again this holiday."

Benny shook his head. "There's no way I'm going swimming in that river! Anyway, how do I know you'll keep your promise. You said we were just coming to the river for a look and now you want to go swimming."

"Because I promise."

"No way."

"Cowardy-cowardy custard . . ."

This time Benny let some of the anger he felt creep into his voice. "Look, Johno, I'm going back to the camp. Are you coming or not?"

Without waiting for an answer he turned and began to walk away. This was his trump card, a kind of declaration of independence and after he had walked some distance he stopped and turned around, confidently expecting to see Johno trailing after him. Instead, his friend had stripped down to his underpants and was standing knee-deep in the water. Benny felt a terrible rush of fear sweep over him. There were crocs out there and if Johno got hurt then he'd have to take

138

the blame. It was no use saying to people, "I warned him", they just wouldn't listen.

"Well, go on then," Johno said.

"Please, Johno, come out of there. Please . . ."

Instead of answering Johno bent down and dipped his fingers into the stream.

"The water's lovely," he said.

"Please come out of there, Johno, it's dangerous."

But Johno kept right on smiling. "Dangerous, is it?" he asked staring round, as if he couldn't understand. "It's only dangerous to cowardy-cowardy custards."

Knowing that he was doing the wrong thing, Benny retraced his steps and went right up to the water's edge. "Come on, Johno, don't mess about, come out of there." He took a step forward, arm extended, meaning to grab his friend by the arm and pull him out of the water, but Johno stepped back determinedly.

"I thought you were going back to the camp," he said.

"We've got to go back together, Johno."

"Well I'll come back with you if you come

for a swim across to the other side."

"No way."

"In that case I'll have to go alone."

He turned and began wading deeper and deeper into the water.

"Johno . . . Wait . . ."

As Benny looked across the river everything seemed more shadowy and frightening than usual. He felt guilty but that was silly. Suddenly all his senses seemed to come alive and he could see right down the river-bed, even amongst the reeds where dark shapes seemed to hide. At the point where he was standing he guessed the river was barely thirty metres across, which was not that wide at all. Surely he could be across and back in ten minutes – at the most? The realization that he was actually going to try made a terrible sickening feeling come all over him.

"I don't want to swim here," he said, knowing Johno could sense he was changing his mind.

"Just there and back, Benny. I dare you."

Benny pulled a face. "I don't want to, Johno."

"Just there and back. No stopping or fooling about." He almost sounded convincing.

"Just there and back? Promise?" He felt weak and helpless at that moment.

"And we won't ever have to come back here again?" he asked.

This time it was Johno's turn to pull a face. "You sound just like my dad. But no. No swimming in the river ever again."

Benny studied the water again: it looked like a dark mirror, smooth as glass. He wanted desperately to see something . . . anything . . . breaking the surface so he'd have a reason to say, "We can't swim, Johno, there's something there!"

The surface remained unbroken.

What was the use of delaying? Better to get the whole thing over as quickly as possible. Wordlessly, Benny began removing his clothes.

"Just there and back, Johno," he said. "No messing around."

Beads of perspiration stood out on his forehead.

"No messing around," Johno agreed, then

turned and dived into the water and began swimming swiftly towards the far bank. Behind him, Benny, quite sick with fear, waded into the river.

Driven by panic he struck out grimly for the other side. After ten strokes with his head down he was breathless and gasping with the effort but his pace didn't slacken. He raised his head only once, saw that in his panic he had drifted off-course and quickly changed direction. When he reached the other side Johno was standing over him.

"See, it wasn't that bad now, Benny boy, was it?"

Panting and gasping from the huge effort he had made, Benny had no strength to smile. He knew only that he had to cross the river again and his racing heart wouldn't slow down. In terror, he stared down at the water, dark and cool as it swept past.

"We have to go back to the other bank now, Johno," he said, clambering unsteadily to his feet. He moved towards the water, eager to complete the ordeal.

Johno ran past him, dived into the water

and headed back. Benny went in after him. Once more the panic welled up inside, stronger, more powerful, this time, threatening to swamp him. He tried to concentrate on swimming in an effort to drive the fear away, but it wouldn't leave. Above the sound of his arms striking the water he could hear the pounding of his heart in his chest.

Halfway across and Johno had already reached the other bank. He was paddling amongst some reeds where the current had pushed him. "C'mon, slowcoach," he shouted and Benny wanted to say that he couldn't swim any faster even if the devil himself were chasing him.

Closer and closer the other shore came. Twenty more strokes . . . then ten . . .then five . . . And it was just when he was starting to feel down for the river-bed with his hand that he felt the first touch: something hard and gnarled had touched his foot beneath the surface. He began to panic and felt his head slip beneath the surface. He swallowed some water. He rose gasping and spluttering, kicking out with all his might. He felt his foot hit something hard and surged forward once again. He looked over his shoulder and saw a dark shape, grey-brown, half-submerged beneath the water. He tried to turn, saw his attacker closing in smoothly at his hip and struck out blindly. Something grasped his ankle and he felt himself being pulled under. He wanted to call out, felt water rush into his mouth and fought bravely towards the surface. Scrabbling to get some hold on the shore, his fingers scraped across the ground. But his leg was trapped in a vice-like grip. Even as consciousness began to slip away he continued to kick out. As he went down for the third time he saw his friend standing motionless on the bank. "Help me, Johno," he wanted to say. "Help me!" Then the blackness took him away.

For a few seconds he lay surrounded by the darkness, wondering. Then, slowly, the awful truth came to him: he had been taken by a crocodile and was now . . . where? In the crocodile's lair? Alive but trapped? The next meal on the menu?

He remembered reading somewhere that crocodiles didn't eat food straight away but

preferred to store it for a time, letting it rot.

Benny felt waves of panic sweep over him again.

Near his face his free hand touched something wet and soft and he became aware once more of the overpowering smell of rotten flesh. He gagged at the thought and then the realization that any movement might bring the crocodile rushing out of the gloomy depths made his heart stop. He had to escape quickly. But how? Suddenly, he was thinking with frantic urgency.

He felt the roof of the small space he was in pressing down on his back. Not even room enough to roll over. The only way out was back into the water, but where was he? What if he couldn't find his way to the surface? And what if he drowned?

But even drowning was better than being eaten alive, wasn't it?

He reached forward again, further this time and touched the water, icy to the touch. Total blackness was all around him. He would have to slide into the water and swim blindly. What if the crocodile was lying silently next to him, waiting for him to move? Or was it waiting outside its lair? Waiting, once more to bite . . .

Benny began to breathe deeply, drawing the stale air deep into his lungs. Once . . . twice . . . three times, then with a silent prayer, he slid back into the water.

On he struggled in the darkness, a roof of roots against his back. Once he held his breath for a full minute and for this reason he had begun to count when he entered the water.

. . . one . . . two . . . three . . .
twenty-five . . . twenty-six . . . twenty-seven . . .
forty-three . . . forty-four . . . forty-five . . .
Then came the crushing pressure in his chest.
forty-five . . . forty-five . . .
Flashing lights began going off in his head.
forty-five . . . forty-five

Images swam before his eyes: Johno; his parents; the river rushing by; and somewhere up ahead light was streaming into the water. The pain that had been building in his head became a crushing weight as he rushed towards the sunlight.

forty-five . . . forty-five

The closer he got, the brighter it became. Bright . . . brighter . . . brilliant.

Wearily, Benny opened his eyes, looking into Johno's anxious face. "You all right?" Johno asked.

Benny hadn't even the strength to reply, though he moved his fist away from his face, and released the stinking reeds he held.

"You got wrapped up in the reeds, I had to drag you out," Johno was explaining. "You swallowed some water. I had to pump the water out of you . . . Wow, but you swallowed a lot!"

Benny saw the triangle of reeds wrapped around his leg and beached nearby a half-submerged log which had drifted to the bank. No bite marks, no blood, no crocodile. Only personal demons, entangled weeds, and a log.

Johno helped him to his feet.

"I think we should go back to the camp now," he said a little nervously and with his arm supporting his friend, led him towards the fence.

The Surprise Symphony

Kate Petty

J. Albert Hall was the youngest member of a frightfully musical family. You might not have guessed that Mr Robert and Mrs Clara Hall were musicians. But by the time you met Wolfgang Amadeus Hall, Johann Sebastian Hall, Andrew Lloyd Hall and Anna Magdalena Hall you would have worked it out. Mother and Father played the piano. Wolfgang played a shiny brass tuba, Johann a polished cherrywood bassoon, Andrew an enormous double bass and Anna the copper kettledrums. They were large children who played large instruments.

So where did J. Albert fit in, small as he was, and Albert hardly the name of a famous musician? The J. in Albert's name stood for

Johann, after Johann Strauss, but you can hardly have two boys in one family with the same name, can you? And Albert? Unfortunately, Albert was his parents' idea of a joke. Albert Hall! Get it? Albert didn't find it funny either.

As the years went by, Albert remained small. Worse by far, he didn't show any natural aptitude for a musical instrument – which is embarrassing when you are part of a frightfully musical family. "And what does Albert play?" asked all the musical friends with smiles of approval all ready prepared on their faces. Father coughed. Mother changed the subject and all the other Hall children said, "Nothing. Albert doesn't play anything, not even the triangle." So Albert felt smaller than ever.

Now you can't live in a frightfully musical household without some of it rubbing off on you. And Albert actually loved listening to music on the radio. He listened to Radio 3 in the daytime and Classic FM if he woke up in the middle of the night. While Clara and Robert and Wolfgang and Johann and

Andrew and Anna were puffing and scraping and banging and making what the neighbours uncharitably called a frightful noise, Albert jammed on his headphones to listen to whatever was on and sat there, tapping his toe and possibly waving a finger in time to the music. Soon he could tell the difference between a symphony and a sonata, a prelude and a fugue, Shostakovich and Schumann. He knew a waltz from a polka and a concerto from a chorale. When the rest of the family said, "Oh, Albert, you're so boring. Why don't you play something and join in with us?" he told them that he was quite happy, thank you. He didn't have to play the music to get pleasure from it. He *liked* listening to it.

This was lucky because at least once a week Albert had to go and listen to the other members of his family performing in concerts. They played in draughty church halls, uncomfortable school halls and unsuitable village halls. Albert sat through them all, nodding his head a little and maybe beating gently with his fingertips on his knee, but often secretly wishing that he could go home and listen to the radio. What he really longed for was to visit a proper concert hall and hear a live performance with professional musicians. He knew it was out of the question. Who could spare the time from such a busy schedule to take him? Who would pay? His mother laughed. "I know it's hard not to be jealous of your talented family, dear, but never mind, perhaps you'll learn to play an instrument soon. As for costly concerts – really, Albert. You'll be asking us to take you to the Albert Hall next!"

Of course, Mrs Clara Hall said this as one of her jokes. The Hall family lived a very long way from London, and a trip to the Albert Hall for the entire family would have been quite impossible. But she had given Albert something to think about. One day an announcement made him sit up and pay attention. Some special concerts were coming soon to the Albert Hall. They were called Promenade Concerts, and tickets cost hardly anything at all if you didn't mind standing! After the announcement they played a piece by Albert's favourite composer – Haydn. Albert wagged a biro thoughtfully in time to the music that no one else could hear.

Albert was a fair-minded sort of boy. It's not easy being part of a frightfully musical family when they are all too busy being talented to take any notice of you. But he was also very determined, and once he decided to do something, then he jolly well did it.

Albert decided that he was going to save up enough money to go to London on a train and hear a Promenade Concert at the Albert Hall. In three weeks' time the Saturday concert would include the Royal Philharmonic Orchestra playing Haydn's Symphony Number 94 – the "Surprise" Symphony – conducted by the famous 91-year-old conductor Ivan Orfolich. That was it!

Albert called in at the travel agent to check all the details of the concert. He worked out how much it was going to cost to get there and planned his journey down to the last minute. Then he told his family that he was saving for a surprise and for the next three weeks he did

any little job that they would pay him to –
carrying the kettledrums for Anna, tuning
the double bass for Andrew, polishing the
bassoon for Johann and shining the tuba for
Wolfgang. He fetched the papers and cleaned
the car, vacuumed the sitting room and put
out the rubbish. After almost three weeks he
added his pocket money and his Post Office
savings to his earnings and he had enough.

When the day came, Albert waited until
Robert and Clara, Wolfgang Amadeus,
Johann Sebastian, Andrew Lloyd and Anna
Magdalena were all practising their newly
polished instruments. He carefully wrote a
note:

GONE TO THE ALBERT HALL.
BACK BY 1 A.M.
LOVE, J. ALBERT

Then he walked to the station which was
just round the corner, bought a ticket and
climbed on to the next train to London. At
King's Cross he got on a number 10 bus which
took him all the way to the Albert Hall.

Summer evening sun slanted across the trees in the park opposite. Albert stood for a moment to look at the great brick hatbox that was the Albert Hall and take in the cheerful atmosphere of the throng of concert-goers. Then he joined a long, long queue for tickets. A friendly couple shared their sandwiches with him.

At last they reached the box office. Albert stood on tiptoe to buy his promenader's ticket and followed his new friends inside. Now, here was some concert hall! Albert looked

round his namesake with pride. How gorgeous the red and gold looked, and how grand! Gradually the huge auditorium started to fill with people. There was a space for the promenaders right at the front. Some people sat on the floor, others stood or leant against one another. Albert found himself a place right at the very front and held on to the rope that separated the audience from the orchestra. He gazed at the empty seats where the musicians would sit, at the music stands, the drums and the cymbals and the organ pipes. He peered up at the conductor's podium that was right in front of his nose. All around him people rustled programmes and chattered until, suddenly, there was a hush. The lights in the auditorium dimmed.

The musicians filed into the spotlight, took their seats and arranged their music on the stands. An oboeist played a single A and then all the musicians joined in, tuning their instruments. People started to clap. The first violinist came on alone, resplendent in evening dress, and bowed to the audience before sitting down. The clapping died away.

And then came a tiny, wizened old man. It was Orfolich. He slowly made his way to the podium. The great conductor turned to face the audience and smiled as they clapped and cheered. Albert held his breath as the hall went completely quiet, Orfolich raised his baton and the first clear notes rang out. Albert lost himself in the music.

"But Albert will get lost in London!" wailed Mrs Clara Hall, quite beside herself. "Robert, you must go after him! Oooh, if only we'd offered to take him ourselves. I should have guessed something was up when he said he was saving for a surprise. Some surprise!"

Robert sat down. "I don't just want to rush off, dear. Let's be calm about this. Albert's a sensible lad. I'm sure he planned this trip very carefully. I expect he's sitting there now, cool as a cucumber, waving his finger around in time to the music." For a moment the whole family pictured the absent Albert affectionately in this familiar pose. "I wonder what they're playing?"

"I'll look it up in the *Radio Times*," offered

Anna. "Well . . . wouldn't you just know it! They're playing Haydn's Surprise Symphony. That's one of Albert's favourites – he once asked to look at my music to see where the drums came in for the surprise."

"I can play that bit on the double bass," said Andrew. And off he went – tum ti tum ti tum ti TUM, tum ti tum ti tum ti TUM; tum ti tum ti tum ti TUM, tat ta ta tum – BANG! Anna played the surprise note on the kettle drum. Mrs Hall squealed. Mr Hall laughed. "That's right, Clara, dear. Haydn hoped that the surprise would make the ladies scream!"

"Robert, how can you be so frivolous when Albert's run away to London? If you hurry you can be there by the interval." Mrs Hall was right. Albert's father ran round the corner to the station, and caught the express train to London. When he got to King's Cross he hailed a taxi to take him to the Albert Hall in South Kensington. He even found himself thinking, as the taxi roared its way past smart people and shops, that the trip was rather fun. He felt quite grateful to Albert.

*

Halfway through already! Albert bought himself an ice cream and squeezed his way to the very front again. He sat himself down on the floor to look at the programme, and read how Haydn had written the Surprise Symphony when he was living here, in London, where he had been a huge success. He'd put the surprise in the second movement to keep the fashionable audience on their toes. Albert couldn't wait to see if the ladies screamed.

After a while some stagehands came on to move the musicians' seats around. Everyone clapped and cheered them. Then the orchestra filed in and began to tune up. The leader of the orchestra took his seat. Then there was a pause. The audience was quiet. People began to rustle their programmes. They talked in whispers. Where was the conductor? Albert peered into the wings. There he was! At last Ivan Orfolich made his entrance even more slowly than before, conserving his energy for the performance, no doubt. He was extremely old after all. But he bowed to the audience with a smile, turned to the orchestra and raised his baton to begin conducting the first movement of Haydn's Symphony Number 94. Everyone relaxed as the sweet notes filled the hall.

The movement came to an end. There was a pause. The audience tensed, waiting in suspense for the second movement to begin and the crash on the drum that would make them jump out of their skins. There were expectant smiles on everyone's faces.

Tum ti tum ti tum ti – CRASH! Too early! A door banged noisily at the top of one of the aisles. A man burst in! "Sshhhh" whispered the people all round him and made him sit down. The audience jumped, the ladies screamed and poor Orfolich tottered backwards into the audience. What a commotion! Everyone rushed forward to help the old man. They pushed and shoved and jostled until Albert was so crushed that he had no choice but to escape under the rope . . . and climb up on to the podium himself.

Standing up there, between the grand orchestra and the grand audience, Albert looked very small indeed. He paused for a moment to straighten his collar and swallowed hard, but he wasn't afraid. After all, he came from a frightfully musical family and he knew how to beat time to the famous second movement of Haydn's Surprise Symphony.

The audience went quiet. Albert raised his ice cream spoon, turned to the string section, and began.

Tum ti tum ti tum ti tum . . . As the moment for the drum surprise came he imagined his sister Anna sitting there, and CRASH! . . . brought the drum in at exactly the right

moment. The orchestra loved it, and so did the audience, none more than the ancient conductor now sitting with Albert's friends eating sandwiches and getting his strength back . . . and a certain Mr Robert Hall, pinned down in a seat at the back as the people on either side of him made sure that he didn't make any more untimely exits or entrances.

Albert was tired. At the end of the movement he clambered down into the audience again as his friends helped Orfolich back on to the podium to carry on conducting as if nothing unusual had happened.

In fact the changeover went so smoothly that people watching the concert on television hardly noticed that there had even been a hitch. From a distance, one small conductor looked much like another. In one sitting room, of course, a family had been aware of every tiny detail. Clara, Wolfgang, Johann, Andrew and Anna sat squashed up on the sofa, their faces streaming with tears. "Oooh, Albert," sniffed Clara. "What a frightfully musical lad you are."

*

The concert finished to tumultuous applause. Orfolich went off and came on again five times. He was presented with five bouquets of red roses. The orchestra stood up and sat down again five times. And then a muffled voice from the back of the hall broke out from the hands that were trying to stifle it and called "Albert!" And the audience took up the cry. "Albert! Al-bert! Al-bert!" they chanted. The orchestra joined in. Orfolich reached down to pull Albert up on to the podium beside him. Holding hands, the two conductors bowed together. Solemnly the ancient conductor presented the small boy with a single red rose. As the audience shouted and cheered, the man at the back of the hall walked up the aisle to the front. "Albert!" he said again.

"Dad!" said Albert, and fell into his father's arms. Robert carried him back up the aisle, out of the door, into the street, on to a number 10 bus, into the waiting train and home into the bosom of his frightfully musical family.

A Bad Day in El Dorado

Gene Kemp

Once we'd got rid of Sharon it was OK, Marie said. We could do what we liked then. Sharon's our eldest sister – fifteen and bossy with it – Mum said we had to stay together all the time we were in the park because you never knew these days with muggers, murderers and worse on the lurk everywhere ready to pounce on the defenceless, even on little Ems – only twelve-months-old – and always asleep except when crawling all over the place, eating everything, anything.

Sharon was mad at this. She didn't want us any more than we wanted *her*.

"Why should I land that horrible bunch every holiday?" she shouted. "It's not fair."

"The sooner you find that life isn't fair the better you'll get on with it," said Mum. "And with me," she added.

"What about my coursework? I've got all the last bits to sort out. It's to be handed in any day *now*. You don't seem to realize."

"You can get on with it when you come back in. You won't be all day at the park. Just make sure you keep an eye on them *there*."

"I used to go to the park on my own. Why can't they?"

"Because things were different then. It's a wicked time today. I daren't let my kids out of sight now. Especially Ems."

My mum's tough with us but Ems is the apple of her eye. Ems can do no wrong, though as far as I can see she doesn't do anything right. If ever there was a juvenile delinquent – I think they call them that – at twelve months – it's Ems. But enough of her.

Mum went. We watched telly for a bit, then Sharon dressed Ems, shrieking and kicking all the way as she hates clothes. Then we set off, Sharon, Marie and me and Ems and Slug. Slug isn't *us* of course. We wouldn't own him

165

in our family, but he's always around because he's an only, living next door.

"Have we got to have him?" groaned Sharon. Slug is called Slug for a simple reason. He looks like one. Pale, oozy and squelchy. His personality does not make up for his looks. That's pale, oozy and squelchy, as well.

"If we don't have him, no one else will," I said.

"So? Can't he just be put down?" Sharon asked, hard as nails from her spiky hair to her booted feet.

Slug wobbled hopefully at us.

"He's coming," said my other sister, Marie, you remember. And Sharon shrugged and left it.

"OK. OK. As long as he doesn't come near me."

So Slug trailed along behind, and I dropped back too, because however yuck he is, and he is, very, at least he's another boy in the female-filled world I live in. You've got an idea what Sharon's like. But *Marie* – well, worse is not the word for Marie. I tell you, at times she terrifies me.

"The pretty one," people say. That's not difficult, what with Ems looking like a Martian and Sharon a gangster. But Marie's all hair and dreaming eyes. She makes up alternative worlds for us; her adventures, she calls them. "I must have adventures. I can't live without adventures," she cries, completely barmy.

Oh, she's nice to me. Not like Sharon. When I was little at school, she'd stick up for me, and she'd fight to her last little toe for any of her family or a friend. But what scares me about her is this:

What will she do next?

What will she get *me* to do next?

Climb our tower block at the end of the street? Go into that empty church that is supposed to be haunted at midnight? Set up on Razor Gillet when he's beating up that kid brother of his, *again*?

You get the message. "Go on, Gary, you know you can do it. GO ON GARY!" And afterwards?

My mother shouting: "And what on earth made you do a daft, crazy thing like that for?"

And when I say, "Marie told me . . ." she doesn't believe me. No one does.

But enough of that. There we were on a warm morning going to the park: Sharon in front, trying to look as if she wasn't with us; Ems asleep in the buggy pushed by Marie (Ems sleeps like an angel all the time it's on the move, the trouble begins if you stop); and Slug oozing along, with me just ahead of him. Somewhere along the way Marie handed over buggy-pushing to me and vanished – to pop up a couple of streets later, whistling happily. She gave me a bit of gum and took over the buggy.

And at the park, who should be waiting there, kicking the bottom steps of the helter-skelter but Mike Andrews, who Sharon's been fancying ever since she got rid of the last one whose name I forget. He turned to watch us as we made our way across the grass and Marie winked one of her great big saucers at me so I knew she'd wangled something again.

"He got here fast," she muttered out of the side of her mouth, in case Sharon heard, but

she was too busy almost not running to where
the beloved stood kicking and grunting at the
foot of the blue and red helter-skelter.

"Love's Young Dream," burbled Slug.

"Shut up," Marie and I both said.

"There I told you," she went on.

"How did you do it?"

"Phoned him, of course. He couldn't get
here quick enough."

"Like I said. Love's . . ." began Slug.

"Shut up," we shouted.

Ems stirred. Marie rattled the buggy a bit.

"We can do what *we* want. Without her . . ."
Marie murmured dreamily. "Come on."

"Where are we going?" I asked, already
scared. "Let's stay here."

"Oh, no. Boring, boring."

"*Where* are we going?"

"El Dorado."

"Oh, no. We can't."

"We can."

"Mum said we weren't to, *ever*."

"She won't know," said my sister, Marie.

She shouted to Sharon.

"We're off, then."

Sharon didn't bother to answer.

"Marie. Slug and I don't wanna go. I like the swings. And the Indian hut. And the pool's full. It's hot. We can go in the pool."

"El Dorado's much better. Besides, I've bought goodies to eat when we get there."

"No."

"It'll be OK, I tell you. It's always OK with me, isn't it?"

"No. It isn't always OK with you. Is it, Slug?"

He slimed up near to us, happy at being spoken to. But Marie smiled into his eyes, which no one ever does to Slug, so he turned dirty orange-mauve and I knew I'd get no support from him. Then she handed him a chocolate drop, which Ems spotted and screamed violently because someone else was getting her choccy drops. So Marie popped one in her wide open gate – sorry, mouth, Mum says not to use "gate" – and began to whirl the buggy across the park at enormous speed, especially considering the wheels which always jam when I do that causing it

to travel sideways or backwards. Once more
Ems fell asleep.

"I wanted to go on something," I shouted,
keeping up.

"Tough."

"We could paddle in the pool."

"This'll be better. It'll be real."

"Pete's sake. The pool's real enough. And
it's hot, now."

"You know what Em is like. She'll want to
go in too and scream the place down. Then
she'll pee in the water and everyone'll be mad
at us. Then Sharon will think she'd better
take some notice of us. We don't want all that,
do we?"

"No," I panted doubtfully. "But do we have
to go to El Dorado?"

Arguing was a waste of time. We pounded
past the adventure playground, the concrete
tunnels, the roundabout, the benches under
the trees, the little houses saying Ladies and
Gentlemen, past the cypress trees and out of
the back gate, down the secret alleyway,
through the back garden of the Four Horse-
shoes and then the dustbinny alleyway at

the back of Razor Gillet's place.

"Quiet here."

And then suddenly we were jumped, shock, horror, even if we were expecting it. Down from the walls dropped one in front, two behind, us in the middle, oh no, it's the end, I thought. Slug squeaked.

But it wasn't Razor. He wouldn't waste time on us anyway, I hope. It was only his kid brother trying to play "menace" with his mates. No match for Marie.

"S–C–R–A–M. Beat it," she bellowed,

charging them with the buggy as a battering ram. As they fled she rounded on the one behind Slug but he legged it as fast as he could.

"RUBBISH," shouted Marie, jumping up and down, slapping her hands. Ems hadn't even woken up.

Then the Pelican crossing, shops on the right, traffic snarling and a gateway in the wall in a corner sheltered by an ancient tree. The gate looked as if it was padlocked but with a twist Marie opened it just as she had the first time. We'd gone again and then once more but that last time someone saw us and told Mum.

Forbidden.

We'd obeyed her. Till now.

"We're there," Marie sighed. "El Dorado."

She twiddled the padlock and we were through. The traffic's noise slid away from us. Sun poured through the leaves into the green valley below. A pavilion/summerhouse thing – oh, I don't know what it's called – glinted gold in the sunlight welcoming us, almost smiling at us as it did when we saw it that first day and Marie called out, "It's El Dorado!"

"What?"

"El Dorado. A place of gold. We've found our 'place of gold'."

"Grub first. Then we'll play."

We found a level spot on the green grass. Ems woke up and we all tucked in. Marie let Slug give Ems her bottle. He turns mauve-orange with happiness if Marie allows him to hold her. It's a nasty sight but it saves time doing it. Then Marie fastened Ems in the buggy and we played, for by then it didn't matter any more that we weren't supposed to be there, that it was forbidden.

We climbed the grey and white stones and rocks, and swung from the rope we'd hung on one of the huge trees growing at the side of the pool. Then we did Marie's version of St George killing the Dragon and rescuing the Princess. Hers is much the same except the Princess (Marie) kills the Dragon (Slug) and rescues me (the Knight). The pavilion place makes a smashing cave for the dragon to come roaring out of, and Slug's not bad at that. He died quite well, too. The pavilion floor's really quite safe, Marie says, though some of the boards are missing. A fantastic place full of treasures – that's where we got the rope for swinging on, and there's an old sofa and a bike and a box full of things like swords – that's how Marie came to think of the Dragon game. The whole valley is full of things, but we're careful. We never play with the old fridge that's been left down here, for instance, 'cos Mum's warned us over and over not to get in fridges and close the doors.

But at last we were worn out, finished, splat. And then I noticed something or rather I noticed a nothing.

"Ems is quiet. Must be asleep," I said.

She'd been screaming blue murder at first because she was in the buggy while we were playing and Slug had worried about her, but Marie popped in a few melty choc drops and she settled a bit.

"I'll get her out of the buggy," Marie said, turning round.

The buggy was empty.

*

I tell you this was one of the all-time bad moments of my life. Marie's face turned chalk-white. Slug made a strange whiffling noise through his nose.

"The pool," he gulped.

We rushed to the pool. Nothing there. Back to the buggy where the reins lay empty.

"I didn't fasten her in properly," Marie said, and a tear began to slide down her cheek.

"She's gotta be somewhere. I know it," I said.

"Ems! Ems! Ems! Ems! Ems!"

El Dorado echoed.

Like mad things we ran through the grass, up and down the hills, round the trees, behind the rocks, crying, shouting, in a dream, no, a nightmare. Ems lost for ever. Mum. Don't think about Mum.

"Ems! Ems! Ems!"

Squawks sounded from behind the old pavilion.

Ems only has three noises and a squawk's one of them.

Like Olympic athletes, we sped towards the

noise. Ems, gurgling and squawking, was attacking a packet of biscuits, just beginning to tear a bit of paper off the packet. Ems was happy. Beside her, cushioned by a mossy bank, her bag of groceries spilt on the ground, lay fat old Mrs Birkenshaw who lives next door, on the other side of Slug.

I stared at Mrs Birkenshaw.

"She's dead," I said.

Marie seized Ems, who shrieked and struggled, then plonked her down with a

biscuit. Ems immediately got stuck into it.

"She's dead," I said again.

"Stop saying that!" cried Marie.

"She looks dead," Slug said.

"How would you know? She can't be dead."
Marie bent over her and shook her
shoulder – she must be brave, I couldn't have
touched the old lady.

"Mrs Birkenshaw, wake up. Come on. Wake
up. You don't want to go to sleep here."

Mrs Birkenshaw did not wake up.

"Ems took your biscuits, but she didn't
mean to, did you, Ems?" Marie went on, her
voice rising higher, and trembling a bit.

Slug peered closely at Mrs Birkenshaw's
face.

"She's an awful colour."

"Even worse than yours," agreed Marie.
"Mrs Birkenshaw!"

"Is she moving a bit?"

"No."

"Some water from the pond?"

"What for?"

"To wake her up."

"I think she's dead."

"No, she's not. She's breathing a bit. Listen."

We listened and looked. Mrs Birkenshaw was indeed breathing a bit, not good breathing but better than nothing at all, a kind of flutter.

"Can we move her?"

We looked at her. A big woman Mrs Birkenshaw, even when on the move. Very big, flat out on a mossy bank in El Dorado with her grocery bag.

"I don't think so."

"We must fetch somebody," said Slug.

"We can't."

"Why not, Marie?"

"And get in a row for being here? We need to move her to the gate and then someone will help. Come on. Everybody find a bit and pull her up."

"No. We can't," I said.

"No. We can't," said Slug.

"I know we can't," said Marie. We stood and eyed one another. Then we eyed Mrs Birkenshaw.

"Just let's go," I suggested. "Somebody's

bound to come along and find her."

Slug looked at me like other people look at him. So I tried again.

"Marie, ring 999 and tell them where she is and we'll push off."

Well, it didn't seem to be a bad idea.

Slug looked at me – even worse. Marie ignored me.

"It's all right," she said at last. "I've thought about telling Mum. It will just have to be done and I'll say it was my fault. I'm going now to ring 999 and I want you to stay here and look after Mrs Birkenshaw and Ems."

"Sharon will get into trouble as well." I tried to cheer her.

She looked at me in a way that told me I was not flavour of the month.

"David," she said to Slug (that's his real name). "I know I can trust you. Watch the old lady. You," she meant me, "try not to lose Ems."

"I didn't lose her last time," I said, but no one was listening, so I turned to Ems who was fine. She'd never been let loose with a whole

packet of custard creams before. Slug sat
with his hand on the old lady's. After a bit he
went to the pool, dipped his hanky in it and
bathed her forehead.

"That won't do much good. Not your rotten
filthy noserag."

He didn't answer.

Marie came back with a police person, Katy
Simmons, who lives two doors down from Mrs
Birkenshaw.

"Hello David. Hello Gary. Hello Ems. Oh,
poor old lady."

She bent over Mrs Birkenshaw.

"You found her here just like this?"

"Yes. Ems found her biscuits. Sorry. You
needn't have let her have *all* of them, Gary."

"What was she doing here, Katy?"

"Well, long ago, there used to be a path
here. It was a short cut. Perhaps she tried to
walk home, felt funny and fell. She hasn't
been mugged."

"Only Ems, with the biscuits."

"Shut up."

I could say nothing right.

"The ambulance is coming," said Katy.

"They can't drive down here."

"No, they'll bring a stretcher. And Marie, what were all of *you* doing down here? Or shouldn't I ask?" Katy had turned into PC Simmons.

Silence.

"There's a NO ENTRY sign and DANGER on the gate," went on PC Simmons.

"It's turned round so you can't see it," muttered Marie.

"Oh, I wonder who did that?"

"I did," said Marie.

"And fiddled the padlock."

"Yes."

Two men with a stretcher came into view. With two others they lifted the fat old lady on it and covered her with blankets.

"Will she be all right?" sniffed Slug.

"Hope so."

"She's a fair old weight," said one of them as they went up the hill.

PC Simmons turned to us, her face very serious.

"I'll tell you what I'll do. I'll put in a word for you and say how sensible you've been and if the old lady lives it'll be thanks to you . . ."

"Oh, thank you . . ."

"In return, you promise never to come here again."

Marie looked all around El Dorado, her eyes more than ever like saucers.

"Not ever?"

"Not ever. Actually the Council has it scheduled for something or other – in the meantime it's forbidden. The whole place could be a death trap. The pavilion's rotten, there's rubbish everywhere, the pool's very deep and they say someone's been dumping chemicals here as well as old bikes, fridges, etc. It's a dreadful place, so keep away. Play in the park."

But the saucers had brimmed over with tears flowing everywhere.

"But it's so beautiful. I love it," wept Marie.

"Why? This old dump. It's awful. Look, Marie, if you love something pretty come and look at my patio some time. I've got lots of flowers and . . ."

But Marie just cried and cried.

"I think you're just scared of what your mum will say," said PC Simmons, turning into Katy once more. "Don't be. Just own up and say you're sorry."

"No, Katy," said Slug. "She's not crying about that. Are you, Marie?"

"Then what are you crying for?"

"The end of magic, of course," Slug said, and Marie nodded as she picked up Ems and fastened her very securely into the buggy.

Goliath

Robert Westall

When I was ten, we went to live in Countess Sikorski's pie factory. We had to. We were poor; my father was an artist, but nobody liked his paintings then. My mother kept us. She was a potter, and loved to make tall beautiful pots, but she never got the chance. Instead, she had to make little ashtrays at five pounds the dozen. With little birds painted on them, and "A present from Bridport". I can see her now, straightening up from the long rows of ashtrays, driving both hands into the small of her back to ease the pain, and staring blankly into space. Thinking there *must* be more to life than ashtrays. But she loved my father, so she kept going.

Mind you, as pie factories go, ours wasn't bad. Don't imagine tall smoking chimneys and miles of grey streets. We lived in the pretty village of Appledown, and the pie factory was a Georgian double-fronted house, though a bit battered and leaky. In front was a cobbled yard, and on each side of the yard were buildings: a coachhouse and stables. In the old stables, my mother made her ashtrays; in the hayloft above, my father painted. And across the yard, in the old coachhouse, the Countess Sikorski made her famous pies, on a long row of gas cookers, some of which must have dated back to Queen Victoria, if not Boadicea. She got the village women in to help, and at the end of a morning, when the huge table in the middle was filled with pies of every size, they would stand in the door of the coachhouse fanning themselves, and wiping the sweat off their red faces with their discarded aprons.

The Countess Sikorski should've been popular; she brought work to the village; she made wonderful pies. Her pies were famous throughout the county, and even today, forty years later, old men will still say a pie is "nearly as good as a countess pie". In her endless search for meat for them, she was the ally of every dishonest smallholder, poacher and black-market butcher for miles around, though she was never arrested for her underhand dealings. People said the Chief Constable was too fond of a countess pie himself . . .

But she could never forget she had been a countess back in Poland before the war, and she never let anybody else forget either. Her husband the count, who had been a colonel in the Polish cavalry in 1939, and a mere lieutenant with the Free Polish Army in 1945, never mentioned it. She had demoted him very much to the rank of private, and he just drove the van that delivered the pies, and as a sideline took illegal bets for bookmakers. He was often arrested for this, but when he came up in court his shy smile, balding head and war record always got him off with a small fine. But when he got home there would always be a screaming row, and the countess would throw old boots and plates at him, and scream that he was dragging the honour of Poland through the dirt. The rows sometimes lasted all night. I got a bit tired of the honour of Poland, though I always enjoyed the thumps and crashes.

The worst thing about living in our half of the pie factory was that it was embarrassing. The countess wasn't one to miss a trick. She had a notice by the gate as big as a billboard.

FRESH PIES FOR SALE. APPLY WITHIN. COUNTESS SIKORSKI PROPRIETRESS.

People stopped to look, in those hungry days of 1946, and the marvellous smell of pies did the rest. But the kids at school cracked jokes. They said the countess put slugs in her pies, and adders, and dead lambs and crows. They said I'd better watch out for our ginger tomcat, or he might vanish one night. In vain I protested she wasn't like that. She loved our cat; she was always giving him titbits. The other kids said she was just fattening him up . . .

To me, the countess was a fabulous monster. Nearly six foot tall, built as broad as

a statute, with a big nose and raven-black hair
pulled back in a bun. She was always slipping
me one of the smaller pies, while they were
still hot, telling me I was too thin, and small
for my age, and unless I ate the pie quick, I
would die of starvation, like so many Polish
children had died. She had no children
herself; or at least she never spoke of them.

But in return for the pie, I had to stand for
hours and listen to her tale of woe; how she
was cheated by dishonest poachers (I never
dared ask what an honest poacher might look
like), thieving farmers, and restaurant-
owners who would not pay what they owed
her. She would say, "Back in Poland, in the
old days, I could have that man whipped or
shot like . . . pouf!" And she would reach out
towards my nose, crack her great floury finger
against her great floury thumb. I didn't mind
listening to her; indeed I felt it was my family
duty, for otherwise she would cross the yard
and go on at my mother instead, as my mother
stood swaying wearily, smiling blankly,
across her rows of unfinished ashtrays. (My
father, wise man, always stayed hidden in the

hayloft with his paintings.)

I suppose she was the devil I knew. The devil I didn't – the other monster of my infant life – was Captain Cholmondely-Bottomley, the Master of the Hunt. Now the kids at school laughed at him as well. For "Cholmondely" is pronounced "Chumley" so the kids worked out that "Bottomley" must be pronounced *"Bum-*ly". So they always called him "Chumly-*Bum*ly" and galloped across the playground jerking their bottoms in the air, in imitation of his riding style, which reduced everyone to howls of laughter.

But although Chumly-Bumly might be a big joke in the playground, outside he was very far from a joke. For the hunt terrified me. First there were the hounds. I met them on the first day I was in the village. My father had sent me for a pint of milk up to Higgin's Farm, and I met them being taken for a walk, in the narrow lane. The huntsman must have been close behind, but I couldn't see him. All I saw was this massive wave of big white, black and brown dogs running towards me – filling the tree-shadowed lane, flowing over every obstacle, blotting out everything. Tongues lolling, big teeth showing, and *all* exactly the same. The same awful hunting sniffing expression, like they would eat anything they met, and the awful feeling they didn't have separate minds like ordinary dogs, but hundreds of bodies and only one mind between them.

They didn't touch me; they only sniffed and licked at me, but by the time the huntsman came into view, I was *screaming*.

Toddy Tyndale, the huntsman was very

good with me; he took me home and explained. Later, he called for me and took me to the kennels to see the hounds being fed. But it didn't make me love the hounds any more. They peed on each other, as they ate; and I was still convinced they only had one dreadful mind that ruled all their bodies.

My father didn't help. He was the kindest man under the sun. A life-long Quaker, a pacifist who had served with the Friends Ambulance Unit in Finland during the war. A man who would literally not hurt a fly; who would get up from his painting and spend half an hour catching a wasp buzzing on the window, so he could release it to freedom. But we were out for a walk one winter morning, when the mist lay low on the ground, and we heard that strange cold haunting note of the huntsman's horn, and they came galloping through the mist, like something out of a nightmare.

My father's hands clenched and he said, almost to himself, "Who do they think they *are*? I know how the archers must have felt at Crecy." I didn't ask him about the archers at

Crecy; his face was too pale and set. But I asked the teacher at school, and he told me that Crecy was a battle against the French, when the English archers killed the French horsemen to the last man and horse, so that they lay piled ten feet deep on the battlefield.

And every time the haunting note came, on a frosty morning, my father would run downstairs shouting, "Where's the cat? Where's the cat?" And there would be a terrible panic until the cat was found, and locked in the hayloft where my father could see him. For my father said the hounds tore apart any cats they found, and our cat was red, like a fox . . .

But Chumly-Bumly himself was worst of all. Another morning, I met him riding at the head of the hunt, and he pointed his riding crop at me, and then at a gate he wanted opening. He didn't say a thing, high on his great horse, just pointed. And after I had opened the gate, silent, terrified, he didn't say anything either, just galloped off. But it was the look on his face. My parents had always looked at me with smiles; so did most people. But I had known kids look at me with hate, before a fight at school, and that *hate* wasn't as bad as the look on Chumly-Bumly's face. He had a thin face, like a hatchet, and his eyes were close together, and the coldest blue I've ever seen. They made me into nothing, as if I was a thing like a fence post, or *less* than a fence post.

My mother said she supposed we had to have the hunt, to keep the foxes down to save the chickens from being eaten. Certainly there were a lot of foxes. Mainly round the countess' dustbins, in the cobbled yard. For they contained everything that did not go in the pies. That is how our cat finally got a name. For our cat knew all about the dustbins too. When he came to the pie factory he was long but thin, and had no name. We just called him "the cat". Then he started the battle of the dustbins with the foxes. And he filled out and finally got a name.

I used to watch him eating there with bated breath, for often the foxes came while there was still some light in the sky.

Now, nobody agrees about cats and foxes. A lot of people say foxes kill and eat all cats.

And cats' skeletons, Toddy Tyndale told me, had been found in foxes' earths, when they dug them out. But there are inexperienced half-grown kittens, and foxes do get them. And there are old cats, and sick starving cats, and foxes do get them. But a full-grown tomcat, with all his wits about him? That's a different matter, I can tell you. Because I've watched. Foxes are smaller than most people think. They're not big wild dogs. They're not much bigger than a full-grown cat, and they hunt and pounce like cats, and live on mice and rats just like cats. They even move like cats, and bat their ears like cats. They're like cats with snouts. And when a cat and a fox meet, they threaten each other and make bullying moves, just like two cats do.

And usually, round our dustbins, the foxes gave way first; and hung about shiftily, at a distance, waiting for our cat to eat his fill. (Usually after the fox had had the bother of knocking the lid off too.)

Until one evening. Our cat was just finishing his supper at the bins, when, quick as light, this fox comes out from behind the wall, and makes a rush at our cat. It was a big fox and it meant to kill and eat our cat. I could tell. I was terrified; I couldn't move or even shout from my window. But it all seemed to happen in slow motion, somehow, so I remember everything.

Our cat saw him just in time. Turned to run. And that would have been fatal. The fox would have bitten him in the neck and that would've been that. But our cat seemed to know that. Quick as light, he changed his mind and got in the gap between two bins, facing outwards. Into the gap went the fox, and out of the gap came a ginger paw full of claws. He hit the fox on the soft bit on the end of his nose, just like Jack Kramer used to hit a tennis ball at Wimbledon. Four times, quick as light. The fox stopped trying to get into the gap, and hastily backed out. He turned and looked round, and I saw the blood on the end of his nose.

But he was a tough old fox, not used to being beaten. He tried again. This time he leapt high in the air, and tried to land on our cat's back.

But before he landed, our cat had rolled over, and had all four sets of claws going like windmills. That fox got what any other tomcat would've got. And he lost his taste for it, as his fur came blowing across the cobbles in the last of the sunset, like red autumn leaves.

He backed off a couple of metres. He and our cat said certain unprintable things to each other. Then the fox turned away in despair . . .

And our cat was after him. Hit him in the middle of the back with all four paws . . .

It was nearly the end of our cat, out there in the open. There was a terrible tangle of red and ginger fur for what seemed for ever . . . then they both turned their backs and walked away. As if they'd agreed it was a draw. They were both limping badly.

I ran out and picked up our cat. He was bleeding in half a dozen places (but so was the fox). Then I heard a voice say, "He is a *hero*! He is like the Polish cavalry charging Nazi tanks in front of Warsaw, with only the banner of the Virgin to protect them! He is a real *Polish* cat!"

I looked up, and there was the countess, beaming at us both, her large dark eyes shining with the unholy light of battle.

"He is a *hero*," she repeated. "We shall call him *Goliath*."

I just stood there, trembling. I thought Goliath was not a Quaker's cat. He had seen death coming for him, and had not turned the other cheek. He had turned four terrible sets of claws, and lived, bleeding, to tell the tale.

If he had turned the other cheek, he would by now be being eaten by the fox, in some hole in the earth.

It seemed a lesson worth remembering. But when my father and mother came out, full of loving concern, and took Goliath off to the vet for treatment they couldn't really afford, I just couldn't look them in the face.

Their Quaker way was wrong. *Their* Quaker way, Goliath would be dead.

Goliath's way, the countess's way, Goliath was alive.

I went to bed in a great muddle. But Goliath healed, and became true king of the dustbins, huge and unchallenged. I never saw the big fox again. I often wondered how he had managed, with no vet to look after *him*.

I remember it was a sunny morning, nearly lunch-time, when we heard the hunting horn, not far off across the fields. My father had come down into the yard to play with me, because he had just sold two pictures, and finished another, and he was pleased with himself, and felt he could waste a bit of time on fun, for once. We were playing a game of our own, with a soft tennis ball and an old baseball bat, that some Yank soldiers had left behind when they left our house after the war. My father threw the ball to me, and I had to hit it to where he *could* catch it. If he failed to catch it three times in a row, I was out. It is a game that only works when played by people who are good friends. . . .

It must have been nearly twelve, because the countess had finished her morning's baking, and the air was full of the delicious smell of pies, and the village women were standing in the doorway of the coachhouse kitchen, watching us idly and fanning themselves with their aprons held loose in their hands.

The sound of the horn grew nearer.

My father said, "Where's Goliath?" His face went as white as a sheet. We ran about the yard, calling for him, looking for him. But he was nowhere to be found. The village women started to join us in hunting and calling; they too knew what the horn meant, and they were all fond of Goliath. But they had no more luck than we did.

The sound of the horn came nearer, while we all stood silent, fidgeting. Then nearer still.

"They'm terrible close to the village," said one of the women. "Don't normally come this close."

The horn again, almost at the end of the village street. Then the hounds making their noise, that terrible brainless sound that means death to any living creature they catch.

And then they came into sight, sweeping up the narrow street, with a small thing fleeing in front of them for dear life.

"That ain't no fox," said one of the women. "It's ginger."

We watched transfixed, as Goliath headed for home with death at his heels. His pride was gone, his beauty. His head was down, his tail was down as he ran blind, without hope.

But he made it to the gate, swept through my legs, and crashed head-on into the corner between the house and the bakery, a heaving collapsed bundle of fur.

And then the hounds swept into the yard.

I did not think. I just found myself standing in that corner over the exhausted body of Goliath. And I still had that big baseball bat in my hand. And the faces of the hounds, the open mouths . . .

I lashed out with the baseball bat. Again and again and again. And I was hitting hounds. I heard my father shout, my mother and the women scream . . .

Something leapt on my back, clawing and gouging me all the way up. Something leapt from my shoulder, clean over the heads of the pack. I will remember the kick of that great leap till my dying day; it nearly knocked me flat.

Goliath landed on clear cobbles. Before the hounds had more than half-turned on him, he leapt again. Straight through the open door of the bakery, straight into the middle of the tableful of steaming pies.

Yet such was his aim, that he landed in a tiny space between two of the bigger pies; he did not disturb a single one.

Then he leapt again, upwards this time, to

the great narrow beam that ran across the roof of the coachhouse; caught it with his front paws, and dangled helpless there for a heart-stopping moment; until he managed to haul himself up on to the narrow beam like a very old man.

Then, gathering his tattered dignity, he turned with all four feet very close together, and spat his disdain and defiance at the pack.

As one, they leapt on to the table in pursuit. There was the amazing sight of pieces of pie flying in all directions.

It finished with the utter disarray of the pack; some leapt unavailingly at the rafter, over and over again, though it was far beyond their reach. Their rebounding feet crushed the pies to pulp. Others, hungry after a morning's hunting, fell avidly to eating the best pies ever baked in the county.

Toddy Tyndale arrived, and could do nothing with them.

Chumly-Bumly arrived, and leapt from his horse, effing and blinding, and laying about him with a whip.

The countess arrived, took one look at her

shattered pies, and grabbed the big yard-broom . . .

Tom Tree arrived at last. He had been the wise village bobby for many years, but the situation was too much even for him.

Mind you, the hounds, weary and full of pie, had lost all taste for the chase. They let the women shoo them out into the lane, with shouts of "Get away, you great dirty things" because some of them had cocked their legs in the bakery.

Toddy Tyndale began getting them whipped-in to go back to the kennels, but he made a slow job of it. Curiously, he kept doubling up against the wall, his back heaving strangely. Then he would throw a furtive glance at Chumly-Bumly.

But Chumly-Bumly had troubles enough of his own. Under the countess's assault with the broom, his hunting cap was gone, his hunting pink was caked with mud from his being knocked flat on to the cobbles and he had a blueing lump on his narrow forehead the size of half an egg. But he was still far too much of an English gentleman to consider offering violence to a lady, even in self-defence.

It was Tom Tree who finally got the yard-broom off the countess.

"Why haff you taken my broom? It is *my* broom, I haff paid good money for it. In England do policemen haff the right to steal brooms? Is that a free democracy? What haff we been fighting the Nazis for, if you can steal my broom?"

"*Madam*," said Tom Tree, as soothingly as possible.

"I insist you arrest this criminal lunatic," she said, pointing a quivering finger at Chumly-Bumly. "He kills harmless pets! He sets his dogs on little children! He has stolen pies to the total value of seventeen pounds, nineteen and sixpence, retail!"

How she managed to work out the exact price while busy belabouring Chumly-Bumly, I shall never know. She added, "In the old days, in Poland, I would have this man *whipped*. I would have him *shot*. Why do you English let your criminals run wild, destroying the pies of honest women?"

"I will pay for the pies," said Chumly-Bumly, stiffly.

"So," said the countess, holding an outstretched quivering hand under his nose. "Where is your money?"

Of course, Chumly-Bumly had no money on him, in his hunting pink. Neither did any of the other members of the Hunt, who were watching on horseback, from a safe distance down the lane, this most un-English of spectacles.

"So. You say you will pay, but you have no money. That is fraud. Arrest this criminal lunatic for fraud. Constable! I *insist*!"

Tom Tree could only shake his head like a baffled bull. After all, Chumly-Bumly *was* chairman of the local magistrates . . .

"Very well, I confiscate this horse, till the debt is paid." And the countess began to lead away Chumly-Bumly's bay hunter . . .

I'm afraid my mother took me away at that point. It wasn't until she got me up to the bathroom that I realized my arms were bitten and bleeding in three places. She washed the wounds and put me to bed, and sent for the doctor. By that time I was trembling all over, and quite unable to lie still.

But then Goliath strolled in, sat on my bed and began to wash himself. He seemed much less upset than me. After a thorough wash, he curled up and went to sleep. I lay and listened to the countess, standing at the gate, telling all and sundry who passed about the Battle of the Pie Factory.

I heard Toddy Tyndall come with the money for the pies, and take away the horse. I heard the Countess shout after him, "I advise you to get a new employer. *I* would not work for a pie-thief!"

I didn't hear what Toddy said in reply; the doctor had just come, and he gave me two injections, that hurt quite a lot.

But not as much as my father's face, when I saw it.

He sat on my bed and said slowly. "You broke a hound's jaw . . ." But it was more than the jaw, which would heal.

He had seen me choose to fight. He had seen me use violence. He didn't have to say anything; it was all on his face. We sat silent a long time. Then he said, "Violence never solved anything, son."

I couldn't say anything back.

I just reached out and stroked Goliath's warm, purring mass.

My father and I looked at each other, silently. We knew. He had chosen his way, and I had chosen mine.

It was never quite the same, afterwards.

Mad Miss Marney

Michael Morpurgo

There is a lost house high up on the moor above Zennor churchtown where no one comes and no one goes. No road leads up to it, and even the peat-black track passes by the front gate as if it might be afraid to go any closer. It looks as if no one lives there for no curtain ever shivers and no smoke breathes out of the chimney. But someone does live there.

Mad Miss Marney has lived on her own up there for as many long years as anyone can remember. In all that time the only people she has ever spoken to are the shop-keepers in Penzance where she goes just a few times a year for provisions. On these rare appearances she is always a source of great interest

209

and speculation for she goes dressed in a coat made from corn-sacks and tied around the waist with binder-cord. She talks to herself incessantly and cackles whenever she laughs. All this may well be why she is known as "Mad Miss Marney". Most people try to avoid her for she is disturbingly strange to look at, but for those who do take the time to speak to her she always has a toothy smile and an infectious laugh that often breaks into a high-pitched cackle.

To the children she is of course a witch. Any bent old lady who lives on her own, carries a wobbly walking sick and cackles when she laughs has to be a witch. But Mad Miss Marney is a witch mostly because the children have all been told to stay away from her by parents who themselves believe that there must be more to Mad Miss Marney than meets the eye.

One of these children was Kate Trelochie who unlike most children had no fear of the dark or of witches or of anything much, but like most children she was insatiably inquisitive. She lived at Wicca Farm under the shadow of the Eagle's Nest. She was an only child whose parents were so yoked to their farm and so consumed by the work of it that they had little time or energy to spare for their child. So she grew up a wild, independent soul wandering the fields and the cliffs with her friends, but always reserving the high moor by the Eagle's Nest for herself alone. The moor suited her for she was a creature of impulsive moods, at one moment unable to contain her exhilaration and at the next so full of despondency and gloom that she could scarcely speak to anyone. Ever since she could remember she had been drawn to the sighing mists and the whispering wilderness of the moor; everything from the collapsed three-legged Quoit, the last sad reminder of some ancient chieftain's earthly sway, to the great granite cheesewring rocks that overlooked Zennor itself – everything was her own private sanctuary, her kingdom.

She loved to be alone up there, to roam free over her kingdom with the wind tearing at her hair. She resented any intrusion – they had no right to be there, it was her place. Leaving the hoof-marked track behind her she would hurdle through the rough heather and clamber over the rocks until her legs would carry her no further. Then she would lie down on the soft spongy grass under the lee of a great boulder and close her eyes and listen to the secret sounds of the moor that spoke only to her – the distant cry of the gulls at sea, the bark of a wandering vixen and the mewing of the pair of buzzards that circled above her.

There was a part of Kate Trelochie that was indeed romantic and dreamy, but the other part was fiercely practical. She came to the high moor by the Eagle's Nest for a specific purpose as well, to hunt and capture specimens for her collection. When she had first come home some years before with a slow-worm wrapped around her wrist, her mother had screamed hysterically and banished all "creepy-crawlies" from the house. But Kate wanted her slow-worm to be warm, and so she kept it secretly down at the bottom of her bed. Other creatures soon joined it in her bedroom: lizards, frogs, toads and even a grass snake. But when the grass snake escaped from his box and ate the frogs, she finally decided that her bedroom was not the place for her collection. So she took over the disused greenhouse at the bottom of the garden and set up her "creepy-crawly" collection and opened it up to her friends – for a price. It was two pence a visit and an extra penny if you wanted to handle the grass snake. She made enough money from the proceeds to buy the nails and the wood and the glass she needed to repair the cages and the greenhouse itself. And she would keep her regular customers happy by bringing back new exhibits from her expeditions on the moor – anything from a mammoth stag beetle to a baby rabbit. The greenhouse came to be known to all the other children as Kate Trelochie's Zoo.

Her mother and father were quite happy about it for it kept her busy and out of mischief, or so they thought. Anyway they admired the entrepreneur in her, setting up on her own like that. They had only one repeated warning, that she was never to go near the lost house on the moor and she was never to talk to Mad Miss Marney.

"She's a strange one," Kate's mother always

said. "Just like her mother was, from what they say. And of course you never know with people like that. It runs in the family. You never know. Just keep away from her, that's all."

Kate had always been intrigued by the lost house and she longed to catch just a glimpse of Mad Miss Marney. Every time she passed the house she would pause and look for signs of life, but the place always looked deserted and empty. She thought often enough about climbing over the fence and snooping around the back of the house, but she thought that that would be wrong – it was private after all. What she needed was an excuse to go and knock on the door; so when just such a chance presented itself, she took it eagerly.

She had spent a long summer's afternoon on the moor trying to catch lizards as they basked on the rocks, but with no success for they were always too quick for her. So she was down-hearted and cross with herself as she began the long walk home down across the moor. She was crossing the track just below the lost house when she noticed something shiny on the dry black soil of the track. As she looked it moved and flapped to life. She froze where she stood and then crept closer. Whether it was a rook or a crow or a raven she was not sure; but it was lying on its side and trying desperately to move away from her using its wings as legs. But the effort of it was too much and the bird keeled over and lay still. It struggled only feebly as Kate picked it up and cradled it to her chest. Angry black eyes glared up at her as she stroked the glistening feathers on the top of his head. She stood for a moment wondering what she should do; and then she felt the blood sticky on her hand. Mad Miss Marney's house was close by and she had the perfect reason to knock on the door – she knew she had to find help if the bird was to live.

The door of the house opened before she had time to knock and standing in front of her was Mad Miss Marney, and at once Kate regretted her boldness for Miss Marney looked anything but pleased to see her.

"What do you want?" she said in a rasping voice. "I've had children up here before coming knocking on my door and running away before I even get there. But I saw you coming up the path, so you haven't got time to run, have you? What d'you want?"

Taken aback, Kate held out the bird almost in self-defence.

"I found this," she said. "And I don't know what to do because it's bleeding. I think it's been shot or something. It can hardly move, but I thought you might be able to help. Sorry if I bothered you."

She was a tiny bent old lady, hardly taller than Kate herself. She leant heavily on her stick and Kate noticed that her finger joints were all swollen and twisted. Her hair, a whispy silvery-white, was pulled up in a bun on her head and the skin around her lips was puckered with age.

"People are always shooting," said Miss Marney. "The things people do for a bit of fun. Don't understand people. Never have done. Come on in, child. Bring it in, bring it in. Don't just stand there. I'm not about to turn you into gingerbread. I would but I don't like it – can't take sweet things any more."

Kate followed her into the house, looking

around her as she went. There were books everywhere. The very walls seemed to be made of books. They stood now in the kitchen, and here too there were books instead of plates on the Welsh dresser.

"Well, what did you expect, child, cauldrons and black cats, pointed hats and broomsticks?"

"No, Miss Marney, honest," Kate lied, and then she changed the subject quickly. "It's bigger than I thought it would be inside, the house I mean. And I've never seen so many books in all my life."

Miss Marney put the bird down on its back on the kitchen table. She spread the wings open.

"It's one of my ravens," she said, almost in a whisper.

There was a tremor in her voice. "Jasper I think it is. Yes it is Jasper, full of gunshot – poor old thing."

"Jasper?" Kate said.

"I give them all names," Miss Marney said, walking slowly past her to put the kettle on the stove. She rolled back her sleeves and washed her hands carefully. "Every bird, every creature on the moor. They are all my friends. I know every one of them – even the ones you take away."

"You've seen me?" Kate was angry at the thought of it. "You've been watching me?"

Miss Marney smiled for the first time – she had very few teeth.

"An old lady can look out of her window, can't she?" she said. "'Course I've been watching you, been watching you for years. After all you came up here more than anyone else and you always have a good look at my house, don't you?"

"But I don't hurt them," Kate protested. "I don't hurt the animals, I just keep them at home and look after them. They're for my collection, for my zoo that I've got in my greenhouse. D'you mind, Miss Marney?"

"No, not if you look after them," Miss Marney said. "Is Jasper for your collection as well, or did you just want to get a look inside the house and see if the old witch is as mad as everyone says?"

Kate was not quick enough to deny it. Miss Marney always seemed to be one step ahead of her and Kate was not used to that.

"I'll look after Jasper," said Miss Marney. "He'll be fine with me. You can come back tomorrow to pick him up if he's well enough and then you can look after him until he gets better. Would you like to do that? It'll be a month or two before he's fit to fly again. But you must let him go when he's better. He won't want to be shut up in a cage for the rest of his life."

"Do you think he'll live?" Kate asked. "He looks so weak, and he must have lost a lot of blood."

"Oh he'll live, child," Miss Marney said bustling her towards the door. "Jasper will live. I have my ways you know. There's not a lot I can't cure if I put my mind to it. Now off you go, Kate, and come back tomorrow."

"But how do you know my name, Miss Marney?" Kate asked, turning by the front door and facing the old lady.

Mad Miss Marney began to chortle and then broke into her witchy cackle.

"Thought you'd want to know that," she said. "I'm not the only one that talks to herself around here. I've heard you talking to yourself up here in the mist. You should be more careful. Voices carry a long way up on the moor. 'Kate Trelochie' you said one day, only a few weeks back I remember. 'Kate Trelochie, you're a genius, a genuine genius. Who else do you know who is only ten years old and has a zoo of her very own?' So you see we are two of a kind you and I. We are mad as hatters, Kate. We love all God's creatures and we love this place with a passion no one else would understand. You are the first person I've had in my house for fifty years and more." She seemed anxious all of a sudden and leant closer to Kate. "You won't tell anyone you've met me will you?" Kate shook her head vigorously. "I don't like people. Don't understand them, and they don't understand me. It's our secret then, just between the two of us."

"'Course, Miss Marney," said Kate, and the old lady patted her on the head and went indoors.

It was a difficult promise to keep that evening with the zoo open as usual and all her friends around her. She longed to tell them all about Miss Marney and her amazing house of books, and she would have done but for a powerful feeling of affection for the old lady. She had been welcomed into a house where no other person had gone in fifty years, and she had been trusted by the old lady to keep their meeting a secret. Tempted as she was she could not and would not tell anyone, but she did go so far as to promise that tomorrow she might have a very special new attraction in the zoo.

"Where will you get it from?" they asked.

"What is it?"

"Can we pick it up like the grass snake?"

"Aha," she said mysteriously to everyone. She knew she had said enough to bring them all back the next day with money in their pockets and so she said no more.

"I saw you up on the moor again this afternoon," said her father that evening after supper. "See you a mile off clambering around in that yellow shirt of yours. Find what you were looking for?"

"Sort of, Father," she said and she smiled to herself.

"Nowhere near that house was she?" her mother asked sharply.

But to Kate's great relief no reply came from her father who was hidden again behind his newspaper.

"You keep away from there like I told you," said her mother. "From what I hear, and I wouldn't be surprised, there's some people say she's a witch."

"I don't believe in witches," said Kate.

"Never you mind what you believe in," said her mother. "You just mind what I say. There's things I could tell you, my girl."

The next morning she was up at first light to prepare a home for Jasper in the old stable that no one used any more. The greenhouse was already over-crowded and anyway she knew enough to know that Jasper and her creepy crawlies would not get on together. She cleared out the old rusty chains and plough shares, the rotten corn sacks and fertilizer bags, and swept it all clean. The hay-rack would make a perfect perch for Jasper when he was better and he would have room to spread his wings. Meanwhile she made a mattress of soft hay for Jasper to lie on.

The mist had come down again as she climbed up into the clouds towards the lost house. Even before she knocked on the front door she heard the old lady talking and laughing to herself at the back of the house.

"Come in, Kate," she heard, and so she pushed open the door and went through into the kitchen.

Miss Marney was sitting in her rocking chair by the stove and sitting on her shoulder was Jasper who cawed unpleasantly at Kate as she came closer. Kate stood astonished. She could see no trace of his wounds. He seemed totally recovered.

"Don't mind him, Kate, it's only talk. Come in, come in – he won't hurt. You didn't tell anyone you'd been up here, did you?"

"No, Miss Marney," Kate said, quite unable to take her eyes off Jasper. "But I don't understand," she said. "He was almost dead yesterday. How do you do it?"

"Almost dead, but not quite," said the old lady. "He'll need some care, some rest and some good food – meat mind you. He likes his meat, don't you, Jasper? Then he'll be righter than rain in a few weeks."

"But how did you do it, Miss Marney?" Kate asked reaching out cautiously to smooth Jasper on the head.

"Oh, I have my ways," Miss Marney said chortling: "I have my ways. I'm quite pleased with him really. To be honest with you I was quite worried when you brought him in, but there's not a lot I can't do if I put my mind to it. Would you like a cup of tea, child? I've only one cup. I've only ever had need for one cup, you understand. But I've had mine so I'll wash it up and let you have a fresh cup. Jasper will go to you, won't you, Jasper? He can't fly yet, so come a little closer so that he can hop onto your shoulder. That's right." The raven put its head on one side and looked warily at Kate, who looked back just as warily. "Go on, Jasper, don't be silly," said the old lady and she jerked her shoulder to get him to move, and Jasper hopped obediently across onto Kate's shoulder. "Quite a weight, isn't he?" said Miss Marney. "Tea won't be long. I've got

the kettle on the boil."

With Jasper balanced on her shoulder, Kate sipped her sweet strong tea and listened intently to the old lady as she sat back, rocking gently in her chair and talked and talked. It seemed as if she was making up for all those fifty years in which she had spoken to no one. She talked of all her animal friends on the moor and of her beloved books. She had read every one of them several times over. She dreaded the cold of the winters she told Kate, for there was never enough money to heat the room and keep the damp away from her bones and the mildew away from her books. Her greatest desire in the world, she said, was for a great warm woolly coat and a hat to cover her ears. Every question that Kate wanted to ask she answered before she could even ask it. Miss Marney was a writer, she said, not a good writer, but not a bad one either. She wrote stories about all the people who lived below the Eagle's Nest, about all the farms she could see from her house, and about the animals and the birds and of course about her moor. But no one would ever read them, she said, because no one would believe them. "They would think they are just made-up stories, but everything I write I have seen with my own eye, my mind's eye perhaps, but I see it just as clear as day."

Several cups of tea later Kate felt she knew and loved the old lady better than anyone else in the whole world, but one thing still troubled her about Miss Marney.

"Miss Marney," she said. "It's about the bird . . .?"

"Jasper," said the old lady smiling. "Jasper. You must call him by his name – it's only polite you know. All right, Kate, I know what you want to know. And you are my friend so you shall know. But you must never tell anyone what I am about to tell you for it is something that people do not understand, and what people cannot understand they fear, and when they fear they hate." She sat back in her rocking chair and sighed sadly. "I have a gift," she said. "I do not know where it comes from, but I have the gift of healing."

"You mean," said Kate, "you mean that you can heal anything you want to? Then what they say is true, you are a kind of witch, a good witch."

The old lady's eyes were closed and she nodded.

"I suppose so," she said quietly. "If it lives I can heal it, that's all there is to it. So now you know my secret. Guard it well my little friend, for if anyone were ever to find out that Mad Miss Marney really did have strange powers, then you know what they'd do, don't you?"

"No, Miss Marney," said Kate.

"They'd put me away, Kate, like they did to my old mother. She had strange powers and they didn't like it so they sent her to a home and she never came back to me. That's why I have never trusted anyone before, why I have never told anyone of my gift, except you. And that's why no one else must ever know."

It was a slow walk back over the moor with Jasper perched heavily on her shoulder. The warm sun had dispersed the mist and the sea was there again. As Kate came down the track towards home she could see that her usual customers were already waiting outside the greenhouse. She managed to dodge around the back of the house without being seen and lifted Jasper up on to his perch before going down to the bottom of the garden to face her clamouring friends outside the greenhouse. She took their money and put it in the biscuit-tin she used for a bank and then led them back into the stableyard.

Once outside the stable with her back to the door she proudly introduced her new exhibit.

"He's the biggest bird in the world," she said. "I found him yesterday, wounded up on the moor, shot to pieces he was – didn't think he'd survive the night. But I brought him back and I nursed him and now he's righter than rain. 'Course he can't fly a lot yet, but he will as soon as he's strong again. He's called Jasper and he's a raven and if you want him on your shoulder it's a penny extra, like the grass snake."

And then she let them in. His size and his presence overawed and fascinated them totally. He was an immediate success. They could not take their eyes off the enormous black bird that sat glaring down at them from the high hay-rack; and once they had seen him perching on Kate's shoulder everyone wanted a turn – at a penny a time.

The biscuit-tin bank weighed a lot heavier that night. Kate knew now exactly what she would do with the money, but wondered how she could ever save enough.

It was little Laura Linnet's mouse that gave her the idea. The next morning she was taking a handful of purloined minced beef into the stable for Jasper's breakfast when Laura Linnet came running into the yard, her face red and smudged with tears. She had a box in her hands, a brown cardboard box with holes in the top.

"It's my mouse," she cried. "The cat was playing with it and I shooed it away but it's hurt and I think maybe it's dead. It's not hardly moving but I thought if you could mend that big black bird then you could mend my mouse."

By this time all Laura's brothers and sisters and cousins were filling the yard, all of them good zoo customers. They were all watching and waiting for her decision. Kate lifted the lid of the box and saw that the mouse was still living. Its eyes were open and it was lying in one corner of the box, its heart beating frantically. Kate's mind was working feverishly for she could see already the opportunities but had yet to work them out. She thought for a full minute, appearing to examine the mouse minutely as a doctor would a patient. Then when her plan was fully formed, she announced to everyone that she could indeed cure it.

"It takes time though," she said. "Always does. I'll have to keep the mouse until tomorrow afternoon. By that time it'll be better."

"How will you do it?" Laura asked, sniffing back her tears.

"I have my ways," Kate said mysteriously. "I have my ways. There's not a lot I can't do when I put my mind to it." And then she added, "It'll cost you five pence though."

Miss Marney was not sure if she would ever see Kate again. She had lain awake all night wondering if her secret might have frightened the little girl away, so she was delighted when she saw Kate opening the gate from the moor and running up towards the house; and she was only too pleased to take in the injured mouse for it meant she would be seeing more of her new friend whose company had become suddenly very important to her after all the long years of loneliness.

"Laura's very upset, you know," said Kate, "and seeing as how you've got the healing powers, I thought, if you don't mind – I thought maybe you could cure it."

"Do you know, Kate, I really don't like mice. I don't know why. But I'll do what I can for anything you bring me," said the old lady setting the box down on the kitchen table and peering anxiously inside. "But no one must know about it. No one must ever know." And she poured out a cup of strong sweet tea again and sat down in her rocking-chair smiling happily. "Do you like stories, Kate?" she said leaning forward. "Shall I read you a story that no one's ever heard before?" She did not wait for an answer, for she knew she did not need to. "I've called it 'The Giant's Necklace'."

It was a ghostly little story and Kate sat

enthralled throughout; but the tea and the story came to an end too soon as all good things do; and with the promise that she would be back tomorrow to collect the mouse, Kate ran back down past the Eagle's Nest across the road and back home to Wicca.

Kate had absolute faith in Miss Marney's healing powers and so she was not a bit surprised that when she went back to pick up the mouse the next day it was running round its box fully restored. She stayed for her tea and her story, this time a strange one about a crippled boy who went to live with the seals, before she made her way back home with the mouse-box.

Laura Linnet and her friends arrived at the greenhouse soon after she got back and when Kate opened the box there was a gasp of admiration and amazement from everyone around her.

"That'll be five pence," said Kate, and then she made her announcement. "I'll be setting up an animal hospital," she said. "It'll be in the old chapel – in secret. My powers will only work if it's in secret. And I don't want anyone else to

know. If they do all the animals I have healed
will just roll over and die. Bring along any sick
animals, any bird, any creepy-crawly. I'll cure
anything you like for five pence a time."

So Kate Trelochie's financial empire
spread from the zoo to a thriving hospital in
the old roofless chapel all hung about with
ivy and brambles and with ash trees growing
up where the altar once stood. Kate would sit
on a granite block under the ash trees by the
back wall with Jasper on her shoulder, and
hold her veterinary court. Several times she
had tried to release Jasper who could now fly
perfectly well, but he did not seem to want to
leave her and she now went everywhere with
him permanently attached to her shoulder.

All summer long the children came with
their egg-bound hens, their limping dogs and
their battle-scarred cats. They brought half-
squashed frogs, crushed moles, torn
fledglings and even a goldfish that could only
swim upside-down and was losing its tail.
Kate took them all in and carried them in
secret up onto the moor to Miss Marney who
would keep them for the night, heal them, and

then return them to Kate the next day when she came for her tea and her stories.

Kate spent most of her days now up in the lost house with Miss Marney, listening to her strangely compelling tales – about the white horse of Zennor, about the milk-drinking knockers of Tremedda. She explored the house and browsed through the books and she talked endlessly to Miss Marney whom she discovered was becoming increasingly anxious as the summer finally came towards its end. She found she was worrying more about her books than about herself.

"It's the damp," she said. "It hurts them, you know, more than it hurts me. Just so long as my books are dry and I'm a little warm, I'm as happy as a lark and then I can write. All I need is a thick woollen coat and a woolly hat to cover my ears. The worst thing about getting old, Kate, is that you can't keep warm like you used to. Up to now I've only been able to write in the summer time. You see, I can only write when I'm warm and happy."

In spite of the success of her animal hospital enterprise, by the autumn Kate had only half the money she needed, and so she came reluctantly to the conclusion that she would have to auction off her zoo. She had nothing else to sell. The zoo was not bringing in much money these days for she had no time now to collect new specimens and everyone had seen the old ones too often. Even the fascination for holding the grass snake was wearing thin. The animals she knew were all replaceable and anyway they would go to good homes. What had to be done, she thought, had to be done.

She held the auction in the ruined chapel and the prices went sky high. Each bid was for a penny so the bidding took some time, but her friends seemed incapable of resisting the temptation to outbid someone else. After all, what was one penny more? Within an hour every creepy-crawly was sold and she had made over five pounds – enough she knew for what she had in mind.

She was just counting her money to be sure, when everyone fell quiet around her. There was the sound of plodding, hesitant hoofbeats and little Laura Linnet came in through the door of the chapel leading her old horse. She had tears pouring down her cheeks.

"The vet's been," she said, "and he says Rubin's dying and he wants to shoot him. He wants to shoot my Rubin."

The horse's head hung almost to the ground and its legs could scarcely carry its weight. He moved slowly into the middle of the chapel and sank heavily to the ground, exhausted.

"I'll pay you anything, Kate," Laura begged. "Just help him, please help him. You must help him."

Kate knelt down by the horse and stroked his neck. He was breathing fast and she could hear a terrible wheezing in the lungs. She could see from the way he sank down that even if she could get him to his feet again she could not walk him all the way to Miss Marney's house on the moor. The faces around her were all expectant, and she knew how popular old Rubin was and that he meant all the world to little Laura Linnet. She stood up slowly.

"I think I can save him," she said. "But it will take time – maybe more than just a day –

and it will take all my healing powers." She needed to give herself room for manoeuvre while she thought things out. "He's very sick," she said. "I've never seen a horse as sick as this. He can hardly breathe."

"But the vet will be back tomorrow morning," said Laura. "Father said that unless Rubin looks better by then, he'll have to have him shot. And he will, he will."

"I'll try," Kate said finally, but try as she did to disguise it there was little confidence in her voice. "But I can't promise anything. Go home now all of you and leave me alone with Rubin. I can't work my healing powers with people around me. Go away and remember – not a word to anyone. Meet back here tomorrow first thing."

They obeyed as they had always done. Kate knew that some of the little ones already thought she was a witch and she used that fear as a threat. Some time ago she had made it known that if any of them betrayed their secret, and told anyone of her healing powers, she had the power to turn them into toads. No one she felt sure would have the courage to put that threat to the test and so her secret was safe.

Kate's mother and father always went to bed early for they had to be up early every morning. She waited fully clothed under her blankets until she heard them stop talking in their bedroom and then crept downstairs. It was a star-bright night with the full moon lighting her way up the tracks towards Miss Marney's house. The first frost of the year glistened on the rocks. She knocked and called out:

"It's me, Miss Marney. Don't worry. It's only me. I need help."

Over a warm welcome cup of sweet tea in the kitchen she told Miss Marney everything, all about her animal hospital in the chapel. She confessed how she had used her healing powers without ever telling her.

Miss Marney listened in silence, her chair rocking back and forth.

"Old Rubin is dying in the chapel, Miss Marney, and I can't do anything for him," she went on. "You must come, I can't get him up here – he's too weak. Miss Marney, you must come – you're the only one who can save him."

"Is it him you want saved, Kate?" Miss Marney asked, "or do you want me to save you?"

"Both," Kate said honestly enough. "But Rubin's the oldest horse around – nearly forty he is. Everyone knows him. Everyone loves him – we've all ridden him. Please, Miss Marney."

"One thing I still don't understand," said Miss Marney looking hard at Kate. "The money. I know you too well, Kate – you'd not make money out of the suffering of animals. What did you want the money for? Tell me that, Kate."

Kate could scarcely see the old lady through the tears in her eyes. "I wanted it to be a surprise," she said. "I didn't want to tell you. I just wanted to give it to you for all the tea and the stories and the nice talks we've had."

"What did you want to give me?" said the old lady leaning forward in her chair and reaching out to take Kate's hand in hers.

"A coat," Kate said. "There's a coat I've seen in a shop in Penzance – a second-hand

shop. But it's warm and woolly and it's only
ten pounds and I wanted you to have it for the
winter. You said it was the thing you most
wanted in the world, so that's why I collected
the money – and I've got enough from the zoo
and the animal hospital to pay for it and for a
woolly hat I've seen as well. They said they'd
keep it in the shop for me – I was going to get
it next week and then this had to happen."

The old lady lay back in her chair and
smiled. "You're a kind little person, Kate
Trelochie," she said, "as kind a one as I'll ever
meet. I'll do it for Rubin, I'll do it for you and
for my warm woolly coat, but I must be back
before morning. I don't want to be seen down
there with you."

Kate put her arms around the old lady and
hugged her, and then helped her into her
corn-sacks and tied them around with cord.
With a last sip of warm tea inside them they
went out into the frosty night and hurried
across the moor hand in hand and down
towards the sea that shimmered silver under
the white light of the moon. And from
Pendeen Lighthouse, the light carved out

its arc over the land and the sea, and seemed to wink at them.

Once in the chapel Miss Marney crouched down over the horse and felt him all over. She looked in his mouth and smelt his breath before sitting back on her haunches to consider. Then slowly, so slowly she extended her hands a few inches above his chest.

"I'll be some time, Kate," she whispered. "You stay by the door and keep watch. And stay awake mind."

But Kate used only her ears as watchdogs and looked on as Miss Marney worked. She did not touch Rubin but knelt over him, her hands held out straight like detectors, and always over the horse's chest. The hours passed and all that could be heard was the sound of the sea, the occasional hoot of an owl and Rubin's laboured breathing, and then she saw Miss Marney take off her sacks and lay them over the horse.

"You'll be cold, Miss Marney," Kate whispered.

"No I won't," she said, and she lay down beside the horse and put her arms around him. "I'm tired, I shall sleep for a bit now. Keep a good look-out and wake me before it's light."

Kate settled down by the chapel wall and pulled her coat up around her ears. To keep awake she tried to count the stones in the chapel wall. Her last thoughts were of the miners who must have come here to pray all those years ago. She wondered what they would think of it now if they came back and found it ruined and deserted.

She woke because she was woken by

someone shaking her shoulder. It was little Laura Linnet. The chapel was filled with whispering children who stood, backs to the walls as far away from Miss Marney as they could. Miss Marney herself was pulling on her sacks.

"You dropped off, Kate," she said, her voice full of fatigue and disappointment. "That was a shame."

"It's Mad Miss Marney," someone said, too loud.

But then Rubin lifted his head from the ground and sat up. He looked around him sleepily, his eyes blinking in the light. He got to his feet easily enough, nuzzled Miss Marney gently and began to pull at the grass beside her.

"Mad I may be," she said. "But your horse is better. Keep him warm and well fed and he'll be all right. He'll go on for more years than I will."

And she hobbled out of the chapel past Kate who was too sleepy to find the words to stop her.

Kate confessed the whole deception to her

friends and offered them their money back. Not one of them would take it – indeed it was Laura Linnet herself who suggested they should all go up to the lost house that afternoon after Kate had bought the coat.

And so a cavalcade of children and dogs and cats and horses and creepy-crawlies in boxes made their way that same afternoon up the black track over the moor to Miss Marney's house. Kate brought with her the bright red woollen coat with a fur collar, and a warm white bobble-hat for Miss Marney's ears. She did not come out at first when Kate knocked. The children all fell silent and listened. They could hear her talking away to herself. Kate knocked again.

"Come in, Kate," Miss Marney called, and they all trooped into the house through the book-lined living room and into the kitchen.

"I've brought your coat, Miss Marney," she said, "I've come to say sorry, and we've all come to say thank you. We've told everyone about how kind you are to animals and about how you heal them and we've told everyone at home you're not a bit mad or witchy. Everyone knows you're a healer now, Miss Marney – the vet says it was a miracle. And my father says he'll be calling on you when his animals get sick. There'll be enough money to keep your books dry."

Miss Marney smiled. "They say," she said slowly, "they say that everything is for the best in this world. But I never believed it, not until now."

And she took the coat and tried it on.

"It's a bit on the large side," she said standing swathed in pillar-box red from head to toe. "But it'll keep me all the warmer. And I like the hat, but I won't put it on now because it'll spoil my hair. Now, children, will you all have some tea? I've only one cup so you'll have to have a sip and pass it around. And if you'll find a place to sit down I'll tell you one of my stories. Some people think I talk to myself I know, but I don't – well not often. I tell myself stories out aloud before I write them down. I haven't yet had time to put this one on paper. It's all about an old lady they once called Mad Miss Marney."

Mozart's Banana

Gillian Cross

He was called Mozart's Banana – a crazy name for a crazy horse.

Most of the time, he was the sweetest-tempered animal in the world. You could rub his nose and pull his ears and he was as gentle as a kitten. But try to get on his back, and POWAKAZOOM! he went mad. Bucking. Rearing. Bolting round the field and scraping himself against every tree.

In the beginning, we all tried to tame him, of course. Every child in the village had a go – until Sammy Foster tore his arm on the barbed wire. Then our mothers all marched up to see old Mrs Clausen, who owned the horse, and Mrs Clausen said: NO MORE. If we went into the field she'd call the police.

After that, no one bothered with him. Not until Alice Brett came.

Alice Brett had never been near a horse in her life. She was a skinny little thing with wispy hair and big eyes, like a Yorkshire terrier, and she'd lived in the middle of a town until then. She looked as if she'd be scared stiff of anything bigger than a hamster, let alone a horse like Mozart's Banana.

Sammy Foster warned her about him, the way he warned all the new kids. On her first day at school, he pulled up his sleeve and waved his arm in her face.

"See that? What d'you think did that?"

He had a fantastic scar. Long and ragged and dark purple. Most kids pulled faces and edged away when they saw it, but Alice Brett hardly gave it a glance.

"Been fighting?"

"Fighting?" Sammy pushed the scar right under her nose. "How'd anyone get *that* in a fight, Mouse-brain? Sixty-nine stitches I needed."

Alice Brett looked at him pityingly, as if he hadn't got a clue. He went red in the face and grabbed her by the collar.

"You think that's nothing? Well, you try and ride that perishing horse, if you're so tough. I bet you ten pounds you break your neck."

He gave her a shake and stamped off. Alice straightened her collar, as cool as a choc-ice, and that evening she was up at the Church Field, staring over the gate.

That was how it began. For weeks and weeks, she leaned on that gate, staring at Mozart's Banana as he trotted round the field. Every now and then he paused and stared back at her with his great, melting eyes. That was all. But she didn't miss a day, rain or shine.

"What are you trying to do?" Sammy said. "Hypnotize him?"

Alice kept her mouth shut and smiled a little, quiet smile that drove Sammy mad.

Then she started coming to the library.

That annoyed Sammy too. He was a favourite with Mrs Grant, who drove the library van. Every Thursday she gave him a special smile as she checked out his books.

"Hope you enjoy them. Let me know what you think next week."

The library was part of Sammy's kingdom, like the school playground and the park. He was always first out of school on Thursday afternoons, and first up to the War Memorial, where the van was parked. No one dared check out a book until he'd looked at it, in case he wanted to read it.

Until Alice came.

She didn't race out of school to be there first. And she didn't scrabble about on the shelves with the rest of us. She walked up on her own, whispered something to Mrs Grant and filled in a little white card. Then she went on up the hill, to see Mozart's Banana.

That was the first week.

The second week, she came back and whispered again, and Mrs Grant felt under the counter and fetched her out a book.

"There you are," she said. "Hope you enjoy it." And she smiled. Her special smile.

Sammy dived out of the van and grabbed Alice's arm as she walked off. "What are you up to? Let's see that book."

"It's mine," Alice said, in her thin, clear voice. "I ordered it. You leave go of me."

Mrs Grant stuck her head out of the van and said, "*Sammy!*" – really shocked – and Alice pulled her arm free and ran away.

The third week, Alice had another book ordered, but this time Sammy was more cunning. He hung around until the van was gone and when Alice came back down from the Church Field he stuck out his foot and tripped her over. She hit the road with a thump and he hooked the bag out of her hand and turned it upside down.

By the time Alice got to school next day, everyone knew she was reading something called *Understand Your Horse*.

We all told her no one could understand Mozart's Banana.

"If you can understand that horse," Sammy said, "I can dance Swan Lake." And he hopped round the playground on one leg.

Alice just listened politely and went off without answering.

Then she turned up at the riding school.

That was Sammy's territory too. His eldest sister worked there, and he fancied himself as an expert – though he hadn't been on a horse since he'd tried to ride Mozart's Banana. When Alice started spending Saturdays at the stables, he was furious.

"She's not paying." He made sure everyone knew. "They're giving her lessons because she helps with mucking out."

He tried to make a joke of it, holding his nose when she went past and complaining about a smell in the classroom. But that didn't bother Alice. She went on quietly doing the same things. Ordering horse books from the library on Thursdays. Helping at the stables on Saturdays. And (of course) talking to Mozart's Banana every evening. Rain or shine.

But, even then, we never thought she'd try to get on his back.

She must have been planning it for weeks, ever since she heard about the Fancy Dress competition. Every year, in Book Week, we all dressed up as characters from stories, and old Mrs Clausen gave a prize for the best costume.

"Suppose *you're* coming as Black Beauty," Sammy said to Alice.

She gave him a long, interested stare. "Good idea. Thanks."

She wasn't joking, either. She spent three weeks working on her horse mask. And when it was finished, she took it up to show them at the riding stables.

Sammy heard all about that, of course.

"My sister said you looked really stupid. After you'd gone, they all laughed at you."

If Alice minded, she didn't show it. She'd got what she wanted, after all. The riding school people had let her borrow a saddle and a bridle as part of her fancy dress. On the Thursday of Book Week, she came into school wearing black leggings, a black jumper and the horse's head mask. With the bridle over one shoulder and the saddle under her arm.

Sammy thought she was going to win the competition and he was twice as nasty as usual. All morning he made snide comments and pulled her hair. Alice didn't take any notice, but, at the start of the afternoon, she went up to the teacher's desk.

"Please, Miss, I feel sick. Can I go home?"

"Oh, Alice! You'll miss the judging."

"I don't mind that. Honest, Miss. I just—"

She looked as if she might throw up at any moment.

Miss Bellamy hurried her off to the Secretary's Office to phone her parents, but there was no one in.

"You'll have to lie down in the staff room," Miss Bellamy said. "Have a little sleep, and maybe you'll be all right for the competition."

"All right, Miss."

Alice sounded as meek as usual. But when we went to fetch her, at three o'clock, she wasn't there. There was just the horse's head, on the chairs where she'd been lying. And a note: GONE HOME.

By then, all the parents were there, to see the fancy dress, and old Mrs Clausen was pulling up in her car. No one had a moment to go chasing after Alice. No one had time to wonder why she'd left the horse mask – and taken the saddle and bridle with her.

Sammy came top in the fancy dress. He always won things like that. Mrs Clausen said he was the best Long John Silver she'd ever seen, and he got a certificate and a book token for ten pounds. He went round showing everyone, and he couldn't wait for school to finish.

"I'm going to take them to the Library van! And show Mrs Grant my fancy dress!"

The moment the bell rang he charged out of school. The van was just pulling up by the War Memorial, and he threw himself into it, stuffed parrot and all.

"Look, Mrs Grant! I won!"

"Well done!" Mrs Grant gave him her special smile – the first one for weeks. "No need to ask who *you're* meant to be. You look wonderful! Just like—"

Then she heard the sound of clattering hooves. We all heard it. Mrs Grant looked past Sammy and her face went dead white.

Mozart's Banana was galloping down the road towards us at top speed, rolling his eyes and snorting. On his back, clutching his mane, was Alice Brett.

She'd done it all by herself. Sneaked up to Church Field with the saddle and bridle. Got them on to the horse while Mrs Clausen was safely out of the way, judging the fancy dress. Held them steady while she mounted. And then—

That's when the madness always hit him. The moment he felt someone in the saddle. He took off straight away, galloping round the field, bucking and rearing.

None of us had ever lasted longer than half a minute. But Alice had stuck on all the way round the field and clung tightly while he jumped the gate. Now he was heading down the hill, completely out of control.

"Into the van!" shrieked Mrs Grant. We all jumped in and shut the door – just in time. The horse went past like a thunderbolt. If we hadn't moved, he would have charged over us.

"Alice is mad!" Sammy yelled. "She'll be killed!"

"Don't exaggerate!" snapped Mrs Grant.

But Sammy was right and she knew it. We all knew it. Mozart's Banana didn't turn at the bend, where the road went round the recreation ground. He jumped the hedge and carried straight on, like a cannonball. Alice was still there when he landed, but she was struggling to get back into the saddle.

There were three more hedges before the railway embankment. A tunnel ran under the embankment and beyond that was the slip road to—

THE MOTORWAY!

We all saw the same picture in our minds. A crazy horse charging under the railway, across the slip road and straight out into six lines of traffic. With Alice on his back.

"We've got to stop him!" Sammy shouted.

"Yes, we must!" Mrs Grant jumped into the driving seat. "Lie down, you lot! And hold on tight!"

She turned on the engine and threw the van into gear. As we screeched away, round the War Memorial and down the hill, we had a glimpse of the school. All the other children were running out to see what was going on. Teachers were shouting and parents were waving their arms about. Mrs Grant didn't waste time on any of them. She stamped on the accelerator and roared down the hill.

As she swung round the first corner, books slithered on to our heads. We were struggling free of them when she swung round the second corner, in the other direction. After that, we decided that lying down was too dangerous. We sat up and held on to the shelves, cheering the library on.

"Hurry up, Miss! You've nearly caught them!"

"He's got to jump another hedge! That'll slow him down!"

The road and the field ran side by side down the hill, for maybe half a mile. We could all see that the van was going to overtake the horse – but what could Mrs Grant do then?

As we drove under the railway bridge, she yelled over her shoulder.

"Get ready to jump out and open the bottom gate! But not till I say!"

I was still baffled, but Sammy had understood. The moment the van stopped, he wrenched the door open and threw himself out. There was a narrow strip of field on our right, between the railway and the slip road. Sammy raced across to the field gate and heaved it open. As soon as it was wide enough, Mrs Grant swung the van round and we went bumping across the field at top speed, with Sammy running behind.

The tunnel under the embankment was meant for cows and it was narrow and dark. Mrs Grant was racing to block it, before Mozart's Banana came galloping through. It ought to have worked. With any other horse, it *would* have worked. The van was in position by the time we heard the sound of hooves. We all held our breath as the noise echoed in the tunnel, waiting for the galloping to slow down. It *had* to slow down. That was the only sensible thing to do.

We should have known that Mozart's Banana was too crazy to be sensible. He didn't even break step. He just gathered himself together and—

"Oh, no!" Mrs Grant said. "I don't believe it! He's going to jump!"

There was no time to do anything. The horse launched himself off the ground in one beautiful movement, jumping higher than any horse I've ever seen, with Alice Brett crouched low on his neck.

He couldn't do it of course. It was an impossible jump. There was an enormous thud, and a horrible scraping of metal on metal as the horse-shoes scrabbled down the side of the van. And there was a soft slithering noise across the roof.

"Stay inside!" Mrs Grant said fiercely. "All of you!"

She pushed the door open and we all crowded into the doorway, to see what had happened. Mozart's Banana was lying on the ground, looking dazed, and there was no sign of Alice. She'd slid right across the roof and landed on the other side.

But she didn't stay there. While we were still gazing at the horse, she came marching round the front of the van, with mud on her face and her riding hat over one eye. She didn't take the least bit of notice of any of us. She marched straight up to Mozart's Banana.

"Well?" she said severely. "Was that stupid or what?"

He looked up at her with big, dizzy eyes and she grabbed his reins and pulled. With one

261

puzzled look, he scrambled to his feet and stood with his head hanging while she told him off.

You don't want to know what she said. If I wrote it down, no one would let you read this story. Even Sammy looked shocked when he reached us.

"*What did you say?*"

Alice just pushed the reins at him. "Hold those."

Then, before anyone could stop her – because no one dreamed, not for a minute, that she'd do anything so stupid – she grabbed hold of the saddle and pulled herself up.

"Alice!" Mrs Grant said. "You can't—"

"He'll be fine now," Alice said. "Come on, you lot. Walk us back to the field."

And that was how we went. The whole crowd of us, in fancy dress. Long John Silver, Mary Poppins, Little Red Riding Hood and two Charlie Buckets. And, in the middle of us, Mozart's Banana, still looking dazed, walking as quietly as a seaside donkey. And Alice on his back, with mud on her nose and a great rip in the knee of her leggings.

We went right past the parents and the teachers and old Mrs Clausen, all the way up to the Church Field. Sammy opened the gate and Alice rode through and slid off the horse's back. She held out her muddy, grazed hand.

"That's ten pounds you owe me, Sammy Foster."

Sammy swallowed hard and stared at her. Then he put his hands into his pocket and pulled out the book token he'd just won. "This OK?"

Alice opened it, nodded and tucked it into her hat. By that time, Mrs Clausen was roaring into the field.

"You stupid girl!" she was yelling. "That's the most dangerous thing I've ever seen."

Alice gave her a long, sad look, as if she knew about things that were a lot more dangerous. "I won't do it again," she said. "He doesn't like it. He hates being pushed around."

Mrs Clausen stared back at her, very quiet. Then she nodded. "Fine. You can come into the field whenever you like."

"Thanks," said Alice.

And she did. She went up every evening and sat on the gate, chatting to Mozart's Banana. But she never tried to get on his back again. He might be crazy, but she wasn't.

And the next time the library van came round, Mrs Grant reached under the counter as we all walked in. "Here you are, Sammy."

Sammy blinked. "I never ordered anything."

"I think someone ordered it for you," Mrs Grant said.

Everyone crowded round to read the title of the book and we all started to laugh. It was *Ballet for Beginners*.

"What on earth—?" Sammy said.

Alice smiled her little, quiet smile. "Time to dance Swan Lake, Sammy Foster."

ACKNOWLEDGEMENTS

The editor and publishers wish to thank the following for permission to use copyright material.

Joan Aiken: for "The Dark Streets of Kimball's Green" from *A Harp of Fishbones* by Joan Aiken, Jonathan Cape 1972. Copyright © Joan Aiken Enterprises Ltd, by permission of A M Heath & Co Ltd on behalf of the author.

Gillian Cross: for "Mozart's Banana" included in *Stacks of Stories*, ed. Mary Hoffman, Hodder Children's Books 1977, by permission of the author.

Helen Dunmore: for "Aliens Don't Eat Bacon Sandwiches" included in *Fantastic Space Stories*, ed. Tony Bradman, Doubleday 1994, pp. 145–62, by permission of A P Watt Ltd on behalf of the author.

Gene Kemp: for "A Bad Day in El Dorado" from *Streets Ahead: Tales of City Life*, ed. Valerie Bierman, Methuen Children's Books 1989 pp. 9–22. Copyright © Gene Kemp, by permission of Egmont Children's Books Ltd.

Judith Kerr: for material from *When Hitler Stole Pink Rabbit* 1971 pp. 45–51, by permission from HarperCollins Publishers Ltd.

Robert Leeson: for "The Sad Knight" and "The Abbot Gets His Gold" from *The Story of Robin Hood*, by Robert Leeson. Copyright © Robert Leeson 1994, pp. 24–41, by permission of Kingfisher Publications Plc.

Rob Marsh: for "Crocodiles on the Mind" and "The Treasure Trove" from *Tales of Mystery and Suspense* 1994, by permission of Struik Publishers (Pty) Ltd.

Michael Morpurgo: for "Mad Miss Marney" from *The White Horse of Zennor and Other Stories*, Kaye and Ward 1982 pp. 83–103, by permission of David Higham Associates on behalf of the author.

Kate Petty: for "The Surprise Symphony" from *On the Run* by Kate Petty, Orion Children's Books 1997 pp. 50–8, by permission of Caroline Sheldon Literary Agency on behalf of the author.

Robert Swindells: for "Night School" 1984, by permission of Jennifer Luithlen Agency on behalf of the author.

Robert Westall: for "Goliath" from *A Walk On The Wild Side* by Robert Westall, Methuen Children's Books and Mammoth, pp. 114–25. Copyright © 1989 The Estate of Robert Westall, by permission of Egmont Children's Books Ltd.

ACKNOWLEDGEMENTS

Every effort has been made to trace the copyright holders but where this has not been possible or where any error has been made the publishers will be pleased to make the necessary arrangement at the first opportunity.